HOLLOW

AMANDA SINATRA

NOTEBOOK
PUBLISHING

First published in 2019 by Notebook Publishing,
20–22 Wenlock Road, London, N1 7GU.

www.notebookpublishing.co

ISBN: 9780993589867

A CIP catalogue record for this book is available
from the British Library.

Typeset by Notebook Publishing.

In loving memory of Noni

CHAPTER 1

I 'm dead. I have to be dead. I don't even remember what I had for breakfast this morning. Did I have breakfast this morning? Shit. But I'm thinking, so I have to be alive, right? Do the dead have their own thoughts? If so, then I'm in my own personal hell. If this is karma for whatever I've done with my time on earth, then I'm not surprised.

Those were the thoughts that went through my head in that first moment. Here I was, possibly dead, and still having an internal crisis. All I knew was that I couldn't feel a thing, but somehow, I could comprehend that my body was lying down. Odd. I was on the verge of totally losing it when I heard something strange. Everything snowballed from there.

"Any moment now," the mysterious sound whispered.

That sound pierced through my inner monologue. It felt like a light switch came on inside me. I entered into overdrive, and it became pretty clear I was lying on the cold, hard ground. The surface below me was rigid and jabbed at my back. *Where am I? Why am I here?* A small fire sparked within me. It started at the top of my head and trickled its way down through my body. Every inch, curve, and surface were touched by the white-hot flames. My bones and muscles seemed locked in place. I could pass as the new Tinman. The fire had me feeling something... so I wasn't dead? I wished I was—the heat inside me was growing unbearable.

Without warning, something stirred in the distance. It sounded like thick boots trekking through dried leaves. The footsteps casted echoes off a wall somewhere—*a building?*—making it sound like fifty or more people were around me. That is, if they *were* footsteps. Now it sounded like heavy drums. Native American drums. But I couldn't open my eyes to look because that would make the pain all too real. My eyelids felt stiff and crusty, which meant I'd been here, wherever I was, for a very long time. I swallowed back some nasty bile and groaned when my throat ignited from the action. Everything was happening too fast, and my slow mind couldn't keep up with all the noises and pains that were coming in all at once. With boots clicking, leaves crunching, fire burning inside me, I finally screamed.

"MAKE IT STOP!"

The footsteps stopped briefly, and then picked back up. My heart hammered faster inside my chest, trying to keep up with the burning in my body. *Am I having a heart attack?* I wondered. *Shit. Now I* am *dying. Well it was a good... uh... wait... how old am I?*

"Yes," the mysterious voice whispered. A voice? It was someone's voice. Someone was with me.

My eyes fluttered open. Standing before me was a tall, dark figure. And that's all I saw, because with the burning came blurred vision, and my heart rate doubled. I began to thrash around uncontrollably as the pain skyrocketed to a hundred. As if the end was near, my temperature spiked like I'd been thrown into a furnace. Sweat poured through my clothes, and it was getting harder to breathe when suddenly, a cold breeze touched my face and loosened fear's grip on my heart.

My body became alert as the pain left me. One second I was screaming in agony, the next I was lying still. My heart slowed down tremendously. Too slow, actually. Not a normal heartbeat for a human. That gave me a weird feeling in my chest. I tried moving my fingers and successfully felt them bend to my will. All the aches and pains subsided and the wind around me began to pick up. Was a storm coming? *Get your ass up!* I ordered myself.

My eyes finally creaked open for the second time. That's when I saw him. The mysterious man stood tall and sure of himself. Waves of dark, curly hair that fanned his forehead ruffled against the breeze. Deep-set, hazel eyes glistened under the street lamp, and his jawline was narrow and covered in five o'clock shadow. Like liquid caramel, the complexion on his face shimmered from the soft glow of the light, and the structure of his shoulders were broad and straight. He wore black boots, pants, shirt, and jacket. This guy was a darker version of Angel from *Buffy*. I chuckled internally and began to sit up. Maybe I shouldn't have been laughing—for all I knew, this stranger could've been my kidnapper. But his appearance was comical. Without hesitation, I looked at my surroundings and noticed that I definitely was lying in the middle of a deserted side street. The closest house was down at the end, and the only thing that illuminated the dry night were four streetlamps on either side of us.

How did I get here? I thought. My forehead was plastered in sweat, and my own hair, which seemed to be tangled with twigs and leaves, stuck to the back of my neck. It was then I realized my body must had been moved prior to my awakening. The thought made me shudder. I set my eyes back on the stranger. He cocked his head to the side and watched me try to adjust to my surroundings. Something wasn't right, I knew that, it became obvious with each passing minute. Whoever this man was, he had to be the reason for my confused mind. The silence between us was deafening, and I became angrier under his stare.

"You. You did this," I accused as I pointed a shaky finger at him.

"I saved you. You should be thanking me," said the stranger. He rocked casually on his heels, a small, mocking smile touched his lips.

I laughed contemptuously at his comment. He honestly thought I should be thanking him? What a fucking moron.

"What happened to me?" I demanded, still fuming from his response.

"A change, and a second chance at life. Come now, I'll explain more once we're out of sight and earshot," he said, turning on his heel toward the woods. The woods? Where was he going?

"Wait!" I yelled. I got up and stumbled toward him. I needed answers now. Why did it matter who heard? Besides, it didn't look like anybody was around but us.

He kept walking toward the woods but slowed his pace. I got my balance and followed him into the darkness. With only our footsteps echoing through the quiet forest, I let my anger subside enough to notice that I could see clearly in the dark. I could smell the birch sap and the earth from beneath my shoes. The air was cool, but it didn't make me shiver. *What happened to me?* Dark orange and vibrant yellow leaves flanked the stranger's side as we neared a stone wall. He jumped over it effortlessly, leaving me in awe. *Wait, how did he do that?* I thought. A slight chuckle carried over to where I stood which made me jump.

"Are you going to stand there all night?" he teased.

"What makes you think I can jump this wall? Are you insane?" I shouted.

"Trust me, you can." *Was he actually serious?* There was no way in fucking hell I could.

"Back up a bit, give yourself some speed," he instructed.

I snorted. "Right." As stupid as it sounded, my curiosity got the best of me, and I stepped a good couple of feet back to give myself a running start, preparing myself to fall on my ass.

I swallowed hard and ran forward, catapulted myself over the wall and gracefully stuck the landing on the other side. My feet were planted perfectly on the forest floor, not a single scrape or bruise from my attempt. I came face to face with him. He looked at me and smirked. "Wasn't so bad?"

"I guess not, but how?" He gazed at me for a long moment and then without another word, he led the way deeper into the forest.

Was I stupid to trust this strange man? Yes. But he was the only one with answers. And why was he so afraid of anyone listening in? The power that had run through me when I jumped made me feel so alive and frightened me at the same time.

After what seemed like eighty years of walking in silence, the woods opened onto a path for us to walk on. Now that it was easier to avoid stepping on huge branches or animals, I got the courage to talk with my... savior.

"Can you at least tell me your name?" I asked.

"Introductions will come shortly. Besides, you wouldn't be able to tell me your name anyway," he replied.

"What the... I know my name! It's..." I paused, *what the fuck?*

"Exactly. We're almost there anyway. Keep up," he said.

How could I not recollect my own goddamn name? Come to think of it, earlier, I couldn't sum up my age. Now my name. Actually, trying to recall any memory of who I was came up completely blank. No matter how hard I tried, my brain throbbed harder with every attempt to remember.

"Why is it every time I try to recall something my head pounds?" I asked in anger. With my pointer fingers, I rubbed my temples and tried to ease the pain.

"Comes with the new life. The less you try to remember who you used to be, the better off you are," he explained.

"Don't you think I have a right to know? Like, I don't know my name, maybe how old I am? That stuff seems pretty damn important to me," I challenged.

He stopped abruptly, which caused me to collide with his back. My head bounced off his shoulder blade and had me stumbling backwards on the path.

"Seriously?" I snapped.

He whipped around to face me, his vacant stare gave me the chills.

"Age doesn't matter in this life. All the ones you loved you forget and die. Now keep up."

His words sliced through me like butter. My chest ached with a hollow feeling and it caused me to tremble. *Age doesn't matter in this life. All the ones you loved you forget and die.* What have I become? He continued down the path without another word and left me with my thoughts. This wasn't right, any of it. I'm alive, yes, but at what cost? I mean, I can't remember, which sucks, and I hoped I would get the answers I deserved, but I couldn't help feeling off about something. Of course, my inner rant was cut short when a soft light at the end of the trail appeared in front of us. The trees fully separated down the straight path, revealing a small brown cottage. Lavender bushes sat neatly on either side of the front door. The grass was a crisp green and a welcome sign hung near the doorbell.

What is a cute little cottage doing out in the middle of nowhere? I thought. As if my night couldn't get any more confusing, the front door swung open to reveal the most gorgeous woman I'd ever seen. Shiny, platinum blonde hair that was pin straight and touched her back side looked like thousands of dollars were spent on it to make it look that beautiful. Any girl would've killed to have beautiful hair like that, including me. Mine currently had leaves and twigs tangled together. Crystal-clear blue eyes like the ocean down south scanned her surroundings until they finally landed on the man in front of her. Soft, fair skin looked delicate to the touch, and dark circles hugged the bottom of her eyelids. Like a model off the runaway, her body was slender, and she hopped gracefully down like an elegant angel to the path to greet the man who'd "saved" me. The energy shifted when she walked. She moved with grace, and the way confidence radiated off her intimidated me to say the least.

"Theodore," she mused, kissing his lips softly.

I noticed she wore dark skinny jeans and white converse. A white sweater was her top attire and a long, silver, feather necklace completed her look. This chick had serious fashion sense.

"Aurora," he replied lovingly.

Aurora? Theodore? What kind of names were those? Not that I could judge because I still didn't know my own damn name. Smacked down in the middle of east bumfuck, I watched their interaction awkwardly as they stared lovingly into each other's eyes. It would've been cute and all if I wasn't so annoyed with the fact that

Theodore still hadn't told me squat about who, what, why, when, and how I got into this situation. I shuffled my feet in the burnt colored leaves and cleared my throat obnoxiously to break up the lovefest happening before me.

Theodore and Aurora both turned to stare at me. No anger or hate in their eyes; in fact, Aurora looked amused.

"Took you long enough to retrieve her, Theodore. I was beginning to think you lost your touch," she joked. Her voice was like wind chimes, delicate once it left her lips.

"I'm not getting rusty yet, so don't hold your breath." He laughed, then turned his body to me and held out his hand. "Are you ready for your new life?"

Was I? When I couldn't even remember my old one? Aurora smiled encouragingly, waiting for me to grab Theodore's hand. I couldn't see anything worse than standing outside by myself like an idiot, and since I didn't have a home to go to, why not? They seemed nice enough, and if they hacked my body into pieces, stuffed me in a bag, and dumped me in the ocean then whatever, because I was alone anyway. Squaring my shoulders, I took Theodore's hand and stepped through the door to my new world.

CHAPTER 2

I entered the cottage and found a whole other world in itself. It smelt like soft pine with a hint of apple cider, and when I turned toward the front windows, I got a lavender scent. It distracted me in a way, almost recalling something from my hollow shell. Theodore dropped my hand and stepped around me, walking over to the fridge and rummaging through its contents. I gazed around the living room, brown couches and a brown coffee table sat neatly in place. A black screen TV was mounted above an old fireplace. The curtains were a soft off-white, and the rug was a nude shade. Everything was brown or black in this room. Nothing hung on the walls except an old-fashioned telephone from what looked to be around the 1900s. Funny how the TV was more up to date than the phone line. I turned my attention to the kitchen where Theodore and Aurora sat at a brown wooden table. A small lavender centerpiece was placed in the middle, and each wooden chair had an off-white cushion on its seat. This cabin was too wooden for me. The kitchen held a fridge, a sink, and some cupboards filled with god knows what. *Weird,* I thought. *This is too modern for a vampire to live in.* Or maybe they decided to morph with the times. My eyes landed on Theodore, who was watching me intensely from his seat. Aurora smiled, but her eyes displayed another emotion.

"Bathroom?" I asked.

"Down the hall, first door on your left," Theodore responded.

I turned toward the hall, feeling eyes on the back of my head, and found the bathroom. It had the same interior as the living room. I closed the door softly behind me and finally took a first glance at my clothes. A dirty white tee, dark jeans, and scuffed up white toms. Did I fall in a ditch somewhere? I brushed off as much dirt as I could before giving up completely. I turned my attention to the square mirror, finally taking in my appearance. At first glance, I had no idea who this person was that stared back at me. Wide green eyes were scared and confused. The softness of her complexion had an off-white look to it, not pasty but close. Dark circles sagged lightly on her bottom lids, and her cheeks had a hint of rose to them. I leaned forward and touched her petite nose, mesmerized by the freckles hidden on top. Her reddish-brown hair was a mess for sure, twigs and leaves embedded in her scalp. This girl stared at me. I stared at her. This was me. With the realization came the pain. My head began to throb uncontrollably. I gripped the sink, muffling my groans so Theodore and Aurora wouldn't hear. My vision blurred. I began to panic until a film-like scene glazed over my sight. A young girl with big green eyes running outside with a kite and a yellow lab. She looked so happy and free. She wore a sunflower dress and her reddish-brown hair was curled at the ends. Why does she look so familiar? She ran barefoot around the yard, laughing and smiling. The sun was bright on her tan skin, and her cheeks were rosy pink. She had no care in the world, just her and her pup.

"Ivy!"

The little girl turned around and ran toward the voice. As quick as the vision came, it was gone. The pain subsided, and my sight came back. My knuckles were white from gripping the sink so hard; I let go and noticed I'd left a crack on the side. What the hell was that? I looked into the mirror and wiped the sweat off my brows, my mind spinning with thoughts of the vision. I couldn't help but feel comforted by it. My gut said not to tell Aurora and Theodore what had happened; they would just think I was crazy. But when I looked down at the damage I'd caused to the sink, it made me realize that something was different about me. Granted, I didn't have one single clue who I was before, but the unsettling feeling washed over me like a bad omen. I wanted answers and I wanted them now. I searched for a hairbrush until I spotted one in the top drawer, then I brushed out the bird's nest on top of my head and stormed back out into the kitchen.

"Care to explain why I have the strength to crack a porcelain sink?"

"Sit."

I slid out one of the wooden chairs, bracing myself for the next words out of Theodore's mouth.

"You must be thirsty. I'll have Aurora fix you up something." He turned his eyes over to her, nodding to give her the order. I bit my lip, waiting impatiently for more.

"Your strength is back. That's a good sign. Usually it takes a newborn a few weeks but your, days. I'm impressed," he said.

I cocked my head to the side, confused as ever. "Not to be rude, *sir*, but what the fuck is going on?" I demanded.

A smile tugged at the corner of his mouth. "Out of all the ones I've created, you're the most sarcastic smartass I've come across. Listen, this information I'm about to give you isn't going to digest easily. I can only give you what I know. Do you understand?"

I nodded slowly, my eyes never leaving his. The nerve of this guy to call me a sarcastic smartass. Whatever. I haven't been the most pleasant either, so I'll take it as long as I can get some goddamn answers.

"Forgive me, this might be confusing at first, but it's the best way I can explain. I haven't created your kind in years, strictly because it's hard to do, and they can die on me so quickly. My last one just happened to vanish. I'm assuming he's dead, but I don't have the time to wait and find out. So, I created you." He paused, watching my expression changed from confusion to an *I have no idea what he's saying to me, but I'm going to play along* face.

"You see, creating a dhampir takes a great amount of precision to master. You can't let them feed too long and you must wait hours, days in your case, to see if they'll make it through the change. Too much blood, they're dead. Too little, also dead. It all comes down to the right amount. On the verge of half human and half vampire." He picked up his mug and sipped gingerly. "Creating a vampire from the beginning is different than a dhampir. It's easier because dhampirs should not exist, but I go against the grain. It gets me in trouble sometimes." He laughed, crossing his arms across his chest.

Aurora came back with the same black mug as Theodore's, placing it in front of me. "It'll help," she said, before taking her seat next to him. I looked down at the liquid, but it wasn't appealing at the moment. My thoughts circled around me. Dhampirs? Vampires? This guy was definitely on something. Vampires were just supposed to be part of the scary stories you tell your kids at night or around Halloween. I had no idea a dhampir even existed, and somehow, I had become one, well "turned" into one. This wasn't supposed to be my reality. But still, I couldn't shake the feeling that he was sort of right. My gut said listen, my mind said nut job.

"The pain," I finally spoke.

"Yes, the pain. You were actually in pain from the first day of the change, but your body didn't register it until the end. Normal for any dhampir," he said.

I sat there debating all that in my mind. Theodore didn't seem threatening, rather, he came off as almost caring, in a way. Aurora was quiet as ever next to him, watching my every action and reaction to Theodore's responses, as if she were afraid I'd lash out. I looked down at my mug again. Realizing how parched I was, I chugged whatever was in there. Tea. Some weird ass herbal tea with a hint of something sweet, I couldn't put my finger on it, and yet, it quenched my thirst perfectly.

"So, I'm a dhampir?"

"Yes. Half human, half vampire. Half alive, half dead. Like I said before, very tricky to produce. Especially in tight circumstances," said Theodore.

"Hmm. And you chose me because?" I asked. I was still baffled that they chose a random chick like myself to become a creature of the night. No, baffled wasn't the right word. Suspicious was more like it.

"Because we saw potential in you," interrupted Aurora.

My eyes met her angelic face. She smiled at me encouragingly, but she was hiding something. It showed purely in her eyes.

"Yes, potential and a new start," Theodore said casually.

I decided not to press any further on that subject and finished the tea in one gulp and slid the mug toward the center. With too much force, it crashed into the centerpiece and shattered.

"I'm sorry!" I jumped up, grabbing the broken fragments.

"It's ok. Don't worry, I got it." Aurora was gone and back in two seconds with a dustpan and cloth.

"We have someone who's going to train you to control that. He'll be here tomorrow," announced Theodore.

Not only am I half dead but, I need to control my new strength.

I backtracked and looked over at Theodore. "Train me? You're not?"

"No."

"Then who are you supposed to be to me?"

"Your mentor."

Aurora came back and put her arms around Theodore, kissing the top of his head. "The sun is almost up. I'm heading to bed. Don't be too late." Turning to me she said, "Theodore will show you to your room. Goodnight."

I nodded my head to her response as I watched her disappear down the hall. Even when she left the room, she held all the attention.

"I'm sure you have more questions. I can answer a few more, but our kind cannot be awake during the daylight hours," said Theodore.

"Just like the books. How strange," I mumbled to myself.

"Yes. A piece of the story that is actually true," said Theodore. Of course he heard me. Another myth that was true along with super strength. Super hearing.

"Does the sun bother me?" I asked.

"Not a lot. You will get a nasty burn over time from exposure, but you can withstand it for periods of time. The true reason I create dhampirs is because I can't do my work during the day. I need a comrade. You will get paid, free room and board, and eternal life," said Theodore.

"So even though I'm half and half, I stop aging?"

"Yes. Certain perks you bring over. But you still have a heartbeat, pulse, can eat human food, and walk in the sun. You're not as fast as a full vampire or strong, but you can surely kick a guy's ass with no problem," he said while finishing his last sip from his own mug.

I pondered that for a bit. All the new information kept swirling around in my head like a pinwheel. *A dhampir.* That's what I was. *Yikes.* Then another thought struck me. No memories. I'd had a vision and yet can't remember my own life. That vision gave me a slight sense of hope that maybe I could regain my previous past self. But my gut still ached when the thought came up. I couldn't tell anyone. Not yet. It wasn't like I didn't trust them, but it wasn't the right time.

"So, I can't remember who I was before?"

"No. When creating a newborn like a vampire or dhampir, you lose those memories. New senses take over, and it basically pushes all the unimportant shit out. Kind of like when you're deleting old emails. You can select all and boom—it vanishes forever. And it's better that way. Trust me," he explained.

Still, I wasn't completely convinced that was all true, for me anyway. Theodore rose from his chair and then, sticking his mug in the sink, he turned gracefully to me with a soft smile on his lips.

"In due time, this will all be a breeze. But for now, I must rest. I advise you to take a little nap, and I also left instructions on your bedside table. Follow me," he motioned with his right hand to follow him down the hall.

I rose from my seat, following in pursuit. Theodore took me to the end of the hall and opened the last door on the right. With a slight flick of his wrist, the door opened to a queen size bed, a window with brown curtains on the far east wall, a mirror, a wooden dresser, and a nightstand with a lamp on it. There was absolutely no cozy feel to the bedroom, and yet, I didn't care. I finally felt the weight of the world on my shoulders and my eyelids seemed heavy. I stepped into the room to get a better feel when Theodore coughed behind me.

A thought struck my mind before he could speak. "What time is it?"

Theodore shook his wrist a bit to expose a fancy watch. "Four in the morning."

"Oh." *Four in the morning?* I thought.

"Would you like to hear your name? Or would you like a whole new one? Of your choice of course," offered Theodore.

My name? That's right. I had a name. Did I want to hear it? Would it make me feel any better? I pondered it for a bit, weighing the pros and cons. The idea taunted me, yet I wasn't so sure if I was truly ready to hear who I was before.

"I don't know," I finally managed to say.

"Sleep on it. Sometimes it takes a while for a newborn to decide. Goodnight," he said, turning on his heel. He was already out the door before I could reply.

Something came over me. My gut was throbbing, telling me to find out. My mind, on the other hand, just wanted to get the fuck to bed. Still standing in the middle of my new room like an idiot, I decided to just go for it. My mouth moved faster than my brain. I ran back out and stopped under the threshold to my bedroom, expecting Theodore to already be in his own room. But no, he was there in the hall.

"I changed my mind. Tell me," I breathed.

He turned in my direction, giving me the side eye. "Ivy. Ivy is your name." Without another word, Theodore entered his room, leaving me in the hallway with a sense that somehow, I'd known all along.

CHAPTER 3

I woke up to the annoying sound of an alarm clock from the right side of my head. I stretched my hand out and swung at the noise; the clock flew off the side table and cracked to pieces on the ground. Oops. Guess I owed Theodore a new one. My eyes creaked open to a soft glow in my room. Since I shattered the alarm clock, I had no idea what time it actually was. From the looks of it, the sun seemed to be lower, almost hidden behind the curtain. How long did I nap for? Did I sleep through the alarm going off all this time? Theodore said the sun wouldn't be that bad but with constant exposure it could be worse. I was thrilled that the curtains were closed but happy some of the soft sunlight still came through. I lay there while my thoughts drifted to last night's event. I still felt empty, like some pieces of my past life really did matter, and my slow heart ached for them back. On the other hand, I was completely calm with the whole idea that I was a dhampir. It was an insane thought, for me anyway, to think any normal person would've been freaked out. But I wasn't normal, and I certainly wasn't a hundred percent human either. Still, there were so many things I wanted to ask Theodore. I wondered if my old self would have been this sane. If she would have been chill with it. Or would she have been one of those stuck up bitches who would've freaked and called the cops. At the end of it all, I was here, and I couldn't really do anything about it but enjoy the ride. What did I really have to lose?

I reached over to the bedside table, grabbing the list Theodore had laid out for me. I'd been too mentally exhausted last night to read it, so now I did.

Instructions:
1. *Your alarm will be set back an hour every night until you are on the proper schedule with everyone else*
2. *In the fridge is a vial of blood. Three times a day, you must take the blood in order to keep your strength.*
3. *Must follow all rules and instructions from mentor and trainer*
4. *NO HUMAN INTERACTION*

The last rule was in red underlined. I must have read the last line four times before I could actually comprehend what was being said. Suddenly, I felt more like a prisoner than anything, but I couldn't dwell on the negatives and remembered I had a second chance at life, according to Theodore. So, if that meant no human interaction, then there'd be no human interaction. Rule number one basically indicated there were others like me, which I didn't know how to feel about. Would I be meeting them soon? I wondered how these other dhampirs had adapted to this weird world. I folded the paper in half, placed it back down on the table, and sat up, arms stretched out, breaking in the new body. Deciding at that point, it would be the perfect time to take a shower. Since I'd just rolled over into bed last night with the same clothes, a hot shower would do me some good.

I hopped off the bed and trekked over to the wood dresser. It held a brand-new pair of jeans and a black V-neck. I scanned the rest of the drawers and finally saw a pair of fresh undies and a white bra. It was almost like they'd been prepared for me. Strange. I didn't know what time it was, considering I'd smashed the alarm clock to pieces, but the way the sun was positioned, I guessed it was late afternoon. I gathered the fresh garments and made my way to the bathroom.

Flicking the light on, I turned the shower knob all the way to hot. I looked over at the mirror again to stare at myself once more. I noticed now that the bags under my eyes were deeper than before. If a human saw me, they would think I was really sick. To me, I just looked run down. I pinched my cheek to try to flush some color there before I dropped my pants down and pulled my shirt over my head. I tossed my old bra and underwear to the side and stepped into the steamed shower. My muscles stung against the hot water, but it soothed them at the same time. I tilted my head back and closed my eyes as the water trickled down my hair and face. I hadn't realized how badly I needed it until I was done and stepped out. I dried off with a big blue towel and put on my fresh clothes. I snagged the comb from yesterday off the toilet top and brushed out my wet hair. Feeling refreshed and semi awake, I tossed the towel over the shower curtain, balled up the old clothes and placed into a pile on the floor and decided to make my way to the kitchen for the vial of blood.

The thought of drinking blood gave my stomach a little squeeze, but little did I know that I would around the corner and find a man sitting at the table. His hands were folded on the wooden surface, and his hair was a slightly messy dirty blond. His gray eyes locked with mine, which froze me in place. The familiarity of them was so strong, I was taken aback by his presence. The air and sounds around us all came to a halt as each second ticked on. The universe, that once rotated around the sun for years, held still in that moment just for us. My mind, body, and soul were claimed by just that one look. That look would forever hold me down, either in the best or worst way, and I was afraid. Our eye contact finally broke when a slight bell sound echoed in his direction. I watched as he reached inside his breast pocket on his jacket where he pulled out a thin phone and began typing away on the screen. It gave me a chance to observe his strong jaw and tight lips. He had scruff on his face, and when he lifted his hand to push his hair aside, I noticed a slight scar near his temple. He wore a black jacket and white tee. His complexion was flawless, and when he spoke, the stunning man held my attention completely. He was gorgeous, and I gawked like a hungry vulture. The beautiful possible vampire or dhampir put his phone down and gave me a smile so blinding, I had a hard time focusing on my breathing.

"Ivy, is it?" he asked.

I nodded, frozen in place. Was this my trainer? I was stunned to say the least. *Why am I acting like this?* I thought. *Why does he make me feel like I'm seeing the sun for the first time?*

"I'm Jackson, your new trainer," he announced. He crossed his arms over his chest. I noticed when he moved, the muscles under his white tee flexed.

"Are you going to sit? Or look like an ice sculpture all day?" he joked.

I snorted like an idiot and sat directly across from him. My cheeks flushed when he smiled his perfect white teeth at me. He leaned forward, his eyes focused on mine. His attention was unnerving, and I found myself leaning in a bit myself.

"I should have told Theodore I was going to be early. Sorry to have caught you off guard," he apologized. I continued to stare at him like a moron. "Theodore mentioned you're pretty vocal about your opinions, yet you seem pretty composed to me," said Jackson. His head tilted, expecting me to respond.

I coughed to clear my throat. My mind swirled a bit by his presence before I found enough courage to speak. "Yeah, I guess. I mean... I don't mean to be rude," I confessed.

He laughed, making me jump in my chair. His voice, his laugh, everything about him had me captivated and on edge. Jackson was the spider, and I had become the fly woven in his web.

"Well, lucky for you, I don't play nice. I'm a hard ass, and I'm not here to fool around," he turned serious. My slow heart skipped a beat when his expression turned cold. *What the fuck just happened?*

"Okay," I gulped.

"I usually don't train newbies anymore, but Theodore wouldn't get off my ass. So, consider yourself honored," he boasted. He did a complete three-sixty with me. Jackson's posture changed as he leaned back and crossed his arms over his chest. His whole demeanor became rigid like ice. It left me confused, and it stung at my heart.

Jackson broke eye contact before heading over to the fridge. He reached inside and pulled out a dark, thick vial of blood. He handed it to me and sat right back down.

"Drink. It's better we sustain our appetite on blood than human food," he informed.

I popped open the cork and the smell wafted up my nostrils. It was intoxicating. I didn't realize how parched I was until my throat began to throb. The vial touched my lips, and I tasted a drop; it was sweet and mouthwatering. Without another thought, I swallowed the entire tube. It ignited my body and warmed my muscles. I felt empowered and rejuvenated. I wanted more. Jackson eyed me before I placed the vial down on the table. I wiped my mouth and licked my fingers until every last drop was gone.

"It can become addicting," warned Jackson.

"I can see why," I breathed, coming down from my high. Now I understand why Theodore had only ordered me to drink three times a day. My first taste of human blood. How odd that my life had come to this. I needed more, but I didn't want to cause an issue already and make Jackson mad. He already scared me as it was.

"After your first full day of being on it, we'll begin your physical training. For now, I will answer any questions you have," he said. He leaned back against the chair. I watched him eye me some more, probably waiting for me to fire off questions. I decided to begin with the basics.

"So, are you a dhampir too?" I asked. The title sounded weird on my tongue.

"Yes. I have been for a very long time."

"How old are you?"

His long fingers massaged his chin as he mulled over his answer. "Hundred and thirty-five years old," he replied.

My mouth dropped to the floor. Holy shit. Hundred and thirty-five years, and I'm barely a day old...I think. I can't begin to imagine what he's seen so far, or experienced. A man with history, and yet he was a complete ass. How charming.

"Do *you* know how old I am?" I asked.

"Theodore said you're obsessed with your age. Does it matter?"

"To me, yes."

"Next question."

"Seriously? What is with you guys with not telling me the truth?"

"I have orders to follow. There are people of higher power in our world."

"Like who?"

Jackson played with the lines on the table, tracing the patterns as his lips pursed in a hardline. "The Imperium Council..."

"I'm sorry the what?"

He rolled his eyes and leaned back into the chair. "Of course Theodore didn't tell you. The Imperial Council is a fraction of the vampire world. A higher power that controls us. There are two other fractions. All that matters is ours."

"And you're not going to tell me what the others are..."

"No. Now, any more questions?"

I weighed different ones to ask in my mind until I finally came across one that had nagged at me in the shower. "Where are we, exactly?"

"Somewhere in a good old New England state. But we're changing locations soon. We tend to migrate to the west. Better tree coverage and food," responded Jackson.

"Oh," was all I could say. Well, that answered that.

"Theodore should be up shortly," said Jackson. "We have to travel at night, obviously. I've come to help as well. And I'm the one with the truck."

"What time is it exactly?"

Jackson picked up his phone and tapped the screen. "Four-thirty p.m."

I looked around and noticed the shadows from the trees danced on the hard, wooden floors. "And the sun is already setting?"

"Daylight saving's time is ending."

"I think I slept through my alarm."

"Obviously."

He seemed annoyed as he said that. He was the hottest yet crankiest son of a bitch I'd ever met. I hoped the others would be different from him. I could picture the outcome between us, and all I saw was fighting and chaos. Yikes. Just my goddamn luck to be stuck with someone like him.

"You're boring for a newbie," Jackson proclaimed.

I flinched from his words. Asshole. "Thanks. You're bitchy for an old man," I retorted.

He eyed me, half a smirk on his face. "Is that all you got?" he challenged.

I don't know why he got under my skin, but I was pissed off. "For someone who's lived as long as yourself, you have a lot of nerve picking on someone who didn't ask for this," I snapped.

"And yet, here we are. I get stuck with a little baby dhampir with PMS," cackled Jackson.

My face flushed a crimson red. I could feel the heat and anger radiating off my soft white skin. I gripped the edge of the table; wood chips fell to the floor. I knew my senses were heightened with this new change, but I couldn't control myself. I felt out of sorts, and he was making it way worse.

"Dude, fuck off!" I shouted.

"Make me," he sneered.

"ENOUGH!" Theodore's voice boomed behind me. I sat still from fear. I loosened my grip on the table, afraid to turn around. Theodore's eyes were slits, cold and angry. His hands were balled in tight fists, and a vein was

popped out from his neck. A hard line had been crossed...
I could feel it, and Theodore was not about it. The
atmosphere in the room changed, and I was beginning to
think I would've been better off dead.

CHAPTER 4:

"Theodore," Aurora said calmly. She approached him from behind, putting her small, delicate hand on one of his clenched fists. The vein that was exposed on his neck subsided, and his sharp stare weakened. It was such a quick action, but Aurora changed the air around us. Her gentle demeanor made Theodore sigh deeply before his eyes fixed on Jackson.

"Waking up to you two bickering is unacceptable. You're grown adults. Act like it," said Theodore.

Jackson's eyes landed on me for half a second before turning back to stare at Theodore's almost composed face. "Sorry. I had no idea you picked up a child."

"Excuse me?!" I snapped.

"We talked about this, Jackson," reminded Theodore.

"Yeah we did."

The air around me seemed to be seeping its way into my lungs, making it harder to breathe. I was overwhelmed with emotions and couldn't quite fathom what was happening in front me. All the tension was circulating around Theodore and Jackson.

"Then do as you're told for fucking once," snapped Theodore.

Jackson jumped from his seat and got in Theodore's face. "Maybe if you kept a better eye on your last dhampir I wouldn't be stuck with this one." He jabbed his thumb in my direction.

"Have some respect, Jackson," said Aurora. She walked over to get in between them.

"I told you I was done training." He snapped.

Theodore pushed Aurora aside gently and grabbed Jackson by the collar.

"I am your elder, and you will do as I say," Theodore stated.

I got up without thinking clearly and rushed to unclench Theodore's grip on Jackson's shirt. With a firm tug, his hands loosened with ease. My strength surprised all three of us as I made Theodore stumble backward with one last pull at his hand.

"Enough, please!" I begged. With trembling hands, I had laid both palms protectively on Jackson's chest. The electricity that sparked between us had me breathless and when I looked up into Jackson's eyes, I could tell he felt it too.

"Start the truck, *now*," ordered Theodore.

Without hesitation, Jackson stepped back from my touch. Without a single look my way, he was out the door where I could hear the engine roar to life. I looked down awkwardly at the floor, waiting for Theodore to scold me. Instead, I got Aurora's small hand on my right cheek. I looked into her ocean blue eyes, waiting for the lecture. She smiled softly at me before taking her hand off my face.

"Theodore usually doesn't get this angry. Jackson is just being a little difficult with his actions lately," explained Aurora.

I bit my lip, searching around for Theodore. He was nowhere to be found, so I turned my attention back to Aurora who was watching me intently by the wooden counter.

"I didn't mean to start an argument. I don't know what I did to make him despise me," I mumbled. Really, I had no idea. It made me feel like an annoying mosquito, and he was just waiting in the wind to swat at me. He aggravated me to say the least, and I was not about being bullied by an old man. If he was that mad about being my trainer, he should take it up with Theodore, not me. But, when I touched him, it was as if I had known of him before. I couldn't quite remember—ironically enough—where we had crossed paths or if we did at all, but in that moment, it felt so right. And that scared me.

Theodore reentered the cabin, and a deep sigh rattled in his chest when he walked over to us.

"I'm sorry," he said.

I could only nod, afraid he would explode again.

He could sense my hesitation. "The bags are all loaded in the truck. It's time we return home."

Aurora reached for my hand, guiding me out the door away from the cabin. I was going to miss the lavender smell, but I was anxious to see the new home. We stepped outside and somehow, between the argument and now, the sky had darkened just enough for us to walk unscathed from the sun. A big black truck was parked in an angle near the house and Jackson was behind the wheel of it. His eyes were focused on something far ahead. I could tell he wanted to avoid me as much as I wanted to avoid him. Theodore took the front seat, while Aurora and I climbed in the back. It was a pretty tight fit, but at least I was behind Jackson so I wouldn't see his face.

Jackson put the truck in drive, and we looped around the cottage. It exposed a secret road I had no idea existed. Through the deep-set forest, we turned onto a weird side road, trees on the right and left for what seemed like miles. I gazed out the window, absorbed by the contrast of the green leaves and the dark road. For any human, it would be difficult to see this detail—for me, it was quite extraordinary. Every other mile, a small house would appear, exposing a deep-set driveway. The backroad became narrower as Jackson drove with ease. Eventually, civilization disappeared behind us.

The thing I noticed about being a dhampir was that time didn't matter. I watched the path twist around a cluster of oak trees, making it hard to see ahead. For what seemed like a good forty-five minutes, the back road widened. It revealed a four-wing, two-story white mansion that covered what seemed like over a thousand acres of rich land. Light posts on either side of the road guided us to the beautiful white building. My mouth became dry from anxiety; suddenly, I was afraid to meet everyone else. Jackson pulled the truck up beside the entrance to the building. I sat stunned, petrified to move.

"It's going to be ok, Ivy," Aurora reassured me.

I gulped and exited from the backseat of the truck. The front door had a cute little welcome sign with two potted white roses on either side of the top step. I hadn't been expecting such a big place. How many others like me were there? Jackson and Theodore snagged the bags from the truck bed, leading the way to the front door. Aurora had her hand placed gently on my shoulder, which helped guide me up each step. I shouldn't have been this nervous, but if the others were anything like Jackson, I had a feeling I wasn't going to last long in this place.

With a swift motion, Theodore led the way inside, followed by Jackson. I trekked in next, taking in the interior. Wooden stairs led up to two side hallways with a soft maroon rug laid on top. The ceiling was high, and the windows were long. Paintings were scattered on the walls, and a small couch area was in the far back right corner. *This isn't so bad*, I thought. I relaxed a bit, curious to know what else this place had in store.

"I will take these bags to our room, and then you and I will go over the details of your job," Theodore said to me. He carried all four bags to the top of the staircase and disappeared down the right with Aurora just behind him.

Jackson, however, had no hesitation and scurried to the left side of the staircase, opening a door I hadn't seen before. I didn't want to stand out there by myself like an idiot, so I made a quick decision and followed him. Why? Because for how he'd acted earlier toward me, I thought maybe some payback would be nice, but I was also a little curious. I opened the door and regretted it immediately.

CHAPTER 5

What the hell was I looking at? Eight pairs of curious eyes stared straight into my soul from a giant black leather sofa in the middle of the room. Their conversation died the moment I made my presence known. It was like being in a room full of statues. I gulped, afraid to even move an inch. Jackson was the first to speak among the crowd.

"Guys, this is Ivy," he said. Jackson leaned against the back wall nonchalantly. His attention was directed toward his phone, completely unfazed by my presence.

"Hey," the others all mumbled.

I nodded quickly and stared down at my shoes, hoping the attention would shift to someone else. *Why did I have to open that door?* I thought.

"I'm Gypsy!" said a petite voice.

My head snapped up to see a long, caramel colored hand reaching toward me. I took it and found a girl smiling at me with brilliant white teeth. Her eyes were brown and almond shaped with long, thick eyelashes. Her hair was black as night and her cheek bones were chiseled to perfection.

"Nice to meet you," I replied as our hands separated.

"You too! This is Tyler and Justin, the twins," she said, pointing to two identical men on the opposite side of the couch. Justin and Tyler both had sapphire eyes and strong builds. Their hair was a midnight black and their complexion a soft ivory.

"I'm Justin," said the one on the right. He wore casual dress pants and a long maroon sweater. He had a prominent jaw line and seemed really sure of himself.

"Hey! I'm Tyler," said the one on the left. He wore a baseball cap, a white tee, and pink shorts. Tyler had a soft smile, and his demeanor was kind. The twins were literally like night and day.

I waved. "Nice to meet you both."

A guy next to Gypsy suddenly spoke up. "Hey, I'm Zach." He had soft, dark brown hair with deep set brown eyes. Tattoos covered his arms, he had a lip ring, and his ears pierced. He was really tall, and I noticed he had big hands when he extended them to shake mine. I obliged and gave him a small smile. *Ok, so they're not as scary as I imagined*, I thought.

Of course, I spoke too soon. Just then, a tall woman with dirty blonde hair appeared and walked over to Jackson. He grabbed her by the waist and planted a big kiss on her lips. *Ouch. Wait, why the fuck do I care?* I mentally shook my head and waited for the blonde's introduction. She swayed in Jackson's embrace and felt him up with her long, manicured nails. Everyone around me looked away, clearly disgusted by the public display of affection.

After what seemed like eighty years of them swapping spit, the blonde turned around with a slight smirk on her lips.

"Ah, the fresh meat. You're adorable," she sneered.

"Ah, Rebecca, the whore," cackled Justin.

"OOOO, BURN!" Tyler shouted as the twins high fived each other.

"You two can literally go fuck yourselves," Rebecca retorted as she flipped them the bird. Then she turned her deadly stare back at me. "I'm Rebecca, and obviously, Jackson is *my* boyfriend."

"Rebecca, nobody cares," said Zach.

"Fuck off, Zach. Sorry Gypsy dumped your ass last month, but don't rain on my fucking parade," snapped Rebecca. Gypsy and Zach exchanged awkward glances before they looked away.

"Knock it off, hon," said Jackson. I watched his hands snake around her curvy waist. She wore tight dark jeans, black heels, and a pink sweater. Her eyes were a soft gray, and her hair was long and straight. She tapped her heel, clearly annoyed with the situation.

"Babe, I was only kidding," giggled Rebecca.

I mentally rolled my eyes, waiting for this useless banter to stop. This whole exchange reminded me of a shitty high school comedy. Rebecca stepped out of Jackson's embrace and cat walked over to me. She eyed me up and down and observed my clothes. Our eyes met and a sly smile played on her full lips.

"I thought you would be prettier," said Rebecca.

"Rebecca," warned Jackson.

"Yeah, that's original," I retorted.

Rebecca gawked at me like I had six heads. "Excuse me?"

"Rebecca," snapped Jackson.

She waved him off before she looked back at me. "I just want you to get a few things straight, sweetie. This is *my* house, and you go by *my* rules. You stay away from *my* boyfriend and you won't get your ass beat, got it?"

"Your house, Rebecca?" said a booming voice. It was Theodore.

We all jumped from his surprising entrance to the room. Rebecca stood there, eyes wider than the sun.

"Th... Theo... Theodore," she stuttered.

"Ivy, come with me please," commanded Theodore.

I glanced back at the group, their faces were stone cold.

"Don't worry, everyone. I'll bring her back," said Theodore before he shut the door behind us.

Things are changing so quickly, I can't keep up, I thought. I felt like I didn't have enough time to process what was happening around me. Theodore led the way up the beautiful staircase with the maroon carpet. I touched the smooth banister as it guided me up to the right wing of the house. Theodore stopped at the end of a lit hallway in front of a carved wooden door. He turned the knob to reveal a small room with a black desk and laptop. He strolled over to the desk and gestured for me to join him as he sat down in a computer chair. I plopped down and waited for him to speak. He pulled out a thick black binder and placed it in front of me. Theodore flipped through a few pages until he found the one he needed.

"Are you ready to begin?" he asked.

I nodded, still a little unsure. "Yes," I replied.

Theodore pointed to the first picture inside the binder. Three different sizes of wine bottles were displayed neatly on the page.

"We run a wine company. With it, we are able to afford living expenses, blend in with society, and still enjoy life," he explained.

A wine company? The fuck? I've gone through all this for some fucking wine? I was dumbfounded. *What kind of vampires run a wine company?* Theodore flipped over to the next page which showed the ingredients of the different wines.

"We sell three different types of our wine. The one common ingredient within the three is vampire blood. Our blood gives it that kick, and the buzz is higher and more enjoyable," said Theodore.

"Our blood?" I questioned.

"Just vampire blood. You will go to our factories and holders to make sure everything is running smoothly."

Theodore flipped a few more pages in before he landed on a set of new rules. The top one was listed in bold letters.

"No human interaction," I read out loud.

"It is crucial that you do your job and you get out. Got it?" he said.

I looked back down at the page, rereading the rules over and over. I could only report to managers of the factories. Other than that, no other human interaction was allowed.

"You will receive a badge and a set of keys tomorrow. Your first shift won't start until after this weekend," said Theodore.

Wait. After this weekend? I thought. I had become a dhampir and an employee for a wine company my vampire mentor owned in the course of a day. On top of that, I couldn't speak to any human, could only drink three vials a day of delicious blood, and I already had an enemy named Rebecca. And to cap it all off, I couldn't remember who I actually was before all of this.

"Thank you, Gypsy, for coming by. Will you show Ivy to her new room?" Theodore asked.

My mind snapped back to reality when I realized Theodore wasn't talking to me anymore. *When did he ask Gypsy to come up here?* I thought. It had to have been when I was deep in thought.

"Of course," Gypsy said.

I got up, ready to leave, when Theodore's last words made me halt at the threshold. "I believe in you, Ivy," he said.

Our eyes connected and I tried to search for answers within them. "Theodore..."

His tight expression softened, "Yes?"

"Why me?"

"I couldn't let you die."

Theodore nodded at Gypsy, and she grabbed my hand and led me out into the hallway with her. My heart wouldn't stop pounding against my chest. One piece of the puzzle was finally placed, and it gave me hope that I was one step closer in finding out what actually happened to me. The other half of me, terrified to know why I almost...died. We walked across the second floor to the left wing where she stopped short in front of another carved door.

"Here is your new room! I'm just across from you, so if you need anything, don't be afraid to knock. New clothes and toiletries are placed on your bed. I'll be back downstairs if you want to come join us again," said Gypsy before she left.

I opened the door and found a twin-size bed, a single window, and a small dresser. On my bed were fresh clothes and feminine products placed neatly on top. I ignored them and walked over to the window and gazed out at the night sky. It was a cloudless night and the backyard was huge. Giant oak trees circled the perimeter. I leaned my forehead against the window and sighed. *Well, home sweet home.*

CHAPTER 6

"Ivy." A slight pounding on my door made me jump away from the window. I trekked over to the door and opened it to find Jackson holding another vial of blood.

"Here, you need this," Jackson said as he tossed the vial at me.

"Thanks," I said. I looked at its thick contents, mesmerized by the beautiful, deep red color. I popped open the cork and downed the sweet liquid. The same familiar rush of adrenaline coursed through my veins, which gave me an instant high. It was then I realized the familiarity of the flavor. The tea Aurora handed me last night contained blood.

"You good?" he laughed.

I chucked the vial at Jackson's head which he gracefully caught. "Are we done here?"

"No. I wanted to apologize for Rebecca's actions earlier," Jackson said while he tucked the empty vial in his back pocket.

I snorted. "Thanks, but I don't need a shit ass apology."

"Okay, well I also came to tell you that in an hour we'll be starting our training," he said.

"Wait. What? Already?" I looked around, frantic.

"Relax, Ivy. You have time," he said.

"I feel like I can't keep up with how much is changing around me," I admitted.

"It gets easier."

"What are you training me for anyways? The Olympics?"

He snorted obnoxiously, "No. You're still half human so you need to make sure your stamina is up to par."

"I'm not weak."

Jackson's head cocked to the side, eyeing me. He stepped forward into my room while I backed up simultaneously. He noticed. "What? Are you afraid of me?"

I watched a slight smirk play on those soft lips. "No... I can never tell what side of you I'm going to be dealing with."

His smile spread like the sun on his beautiful face. He continued to walk toward me as I backed up farther. Eventually, my body was pressed hard against the window, and his god-like stature was inches from mine. He placed both his hands on either side of the wall. I was pinned directly in the middle, staring at this gorgeous man. My mouth became dry, and my palms were clammy from how close he was to me. I could see every detail on his face that I hadn't noticed before. Slight freckles kissed his nose and cheeks, and I could faintly see some stubble on his chin.

"Scared of me now?" he breathed. The smell of cool mint and sugar tickled my face. It was heavenly, and I wanted to lean in and taste his mouth. *What the fuck, Ivy?* I thought. *Get your shit together.*

My mouth inches from his had me trembling for some air. "No," I whispered.

"Ivy..."

"Babe! Where are you?"

The sound of that female voice broke our private bubble of tension instantly. Jackson jumped back from me while I gulped for some air. Desire lingered in his eyes, but it quickly faded when the footsteps got closer to us.

What was that? I thought. One minute he hated me, the next he was barely inches from my lips. Granted I did the same, but he had a girlfriend. *Oh my god what is going on with me?* I shook my myself and wiped my overly clammy hands on my jeans. Seconds later, Rebecca emerged from the hallway in short shorts and a small tank top showing her midriff.

"You lost, little Ivy?" Rebecca teased.

"This is *my* room, Rebecca," I reminded her.

"Rebecca, knock it off. I was just giving Ivy her food," interrupted Jackson.

"Well, it's time for bed," she announced.

"I told you I won't be sleeping with you tonight. I have to train Ivy," he said.

"I don't understand why you can't wait until later to train her skinny ass," she sneered.

"The sooner I train her, the better," he said.

"Well, come cuddle me until it's time to go. I'll be in my room waiting," Rebecca stomped off without another word or look in my direction.

That girl has major issues, I thought.

Jackson stood still for what seemed like forever. I watched his muscles tense under his shirt as he sighed deeply.

"Jackson..."

"I'll grab you in an hour. Be ready," he said. He walked out, the smell of his cologne lingering in the air.

I stood there, dumbfounded. Jackson. Jackson and I. Shit.

CHAPTER 7

*J*ackson, I thought, touching my lips as if he'd already stolen a kiss. I pressed my head against the window, trying to recollect myself. Closing my eyes, I breathed in deeply through my nose and waited for the rush of hot desire to leave my body. This was all wrong.

"You look rough."

I jumped and turned around to stare directly at Gypsy. She was leaning casually on the doorframe with a smirk on her face.

"Does anyone know what privacy means in this place?" I snapped.

"Woah, girl. It's okay. I was just heading to bed. Remember, my room is across from yours?" Gypsy said as she thumbed the door behind her. I took in her outfit and realized she was indeed ready for bed.

"Sorry." I walked over to my bed, knocked the toiletries on the floor and slumped down, exhausted with defeat. My room was like a revolving door, when one person left, another slithered right in without warning.

"Ivy?"

"Yeah?"

"If you want to talk, I'm here for you. I know what it's like," said Gypsy.

I contemplated this. *Would it be so bad if Gypsy knew everything?* I thought. *Would she understand?* Her brown eyes showed kindness and understanding. What else could go wrong besides her calling me a freak? I sat up and patted the seat next to me on the bed. Gypsy walked in, shut the door behind her, and hopped on the bed next to me. I stared down at my palms and looked them over and over until I could recollect my thoughts. *Where do I even begin?* After what seemed like an endless silence between us, I took a deep breath and released all the stuff I'd been keeping inside.

"Gypsy, I think I had a vision of my past," I finally said.

Her beautiful brown eyes grew wide. "Wait, really?"

"Yeah," I mumbled. Maybe this would help alleviate the heavy weight on my shoulders.

Gypsy surprised me by grabbing my hand. "I'm here. It's okay."

I swallowed a hard lump in my throat. "When I woke, Theodore said it was normal for me not to remember anything. I thought I was robbed. I was angry. When we arrived at the cottage, I asked to use the bathroom that's when..." The memory of the pain came flooding back.

"Ivy?" said Gypsy.

I let go of Gypsy's hand and played with a few strands of my hair. "that's when I saw my reflection in the mirror... it hurt. Some type of vision or flashback came through, and I saw a young girl who looked like me running around. It was all so strange," I finished.

Gypsy surprised me by jumping up from the bed. She paced back and forth, tapping her long caramel finger on her chin. Then she turned to me with a big smile on her face and, clapping her hands, grabbed me by the wrists.

"Ivy! I want to help you. This is obviously super important, and it definitely means something. No other dhampir I know of since I've been changed has had this. This could be our chance to uncover some truth to our previous lives," said Gypsy.

"I just want to keep this between us. I don't want to have any more issues, especially with Rebecca," I said.

"I promise! And please, Rebecca is the skankiest dhampir that ever lived. Her small brain has a hard time counting sheep," laughed Gypsy.

I giggled and sat back down on the bed. "Well, she clearly proved her point tonight with her bedtime outfit."

"WHAT!" gasped Gypsy.

"Yeah Jackson came in to give me dinner and..." I paused. My cheeks flushed at the intimate memory between us.

"Oh my god."

"No... I don't know. He acted so weird with me," I finally said.

"Like how?" asked Gypsy.

"He was all up in my personal bubble. I thought he was going to kiss me!" I exclaimed.

Gypsy smiled at me before sitting back down on the bed next to me. "Girl, anyone with eyes could see how Jackson was staring at you downstairs."

"What?"

"I don't know what you did, but Jackson is completely smitten with you, and he's trying so hard to hide it. It's only a matter of time before he realizes you're the better choice," she laughed.

"It's wrong. He's with Rebecca. I shouldn't even be thinking about him in that way."

I looked down at my small hands, thinking over everything that was said between Gypsy and I. I had shared one of my biggest secrets with her and I felt so relieved that she hadn't judged me. On the other hand, my gut still had me feeling off about everything to do with the vision and what it actually meant. If I had more, maybe I could figure out why I was turned and who I was before. I was still trying to come to terms with my new, crazy life. Now, I had Jackson maybe possibly having some kind of feelings for me. It gave me a thrill to think about, and that scared me. Was it smart to like him? No, he was with someone else. As much as I disliked Rebecca, that was another woman's man. I realized Gypsy was still beside me on the bed and probably watching all my facial expressions. With a small smile, I looked over at her.

"I just need to understand how to be a dhampir first," I admitted.

"And you will. I will help you. I know this sounds silly, but I haven't had a friend in a long time, and when I met you earlier, I felt a connection with you," said Gypsy.

I reached over and gave her a hug. "Thank you, it really means a lot."

"Hey! What are friends for?"

"Well, you're my first one so far."

"Don't worry, everyone else is nice,"

"How many more of us are there?"

"There's nine of us in total."

Just then, a hard knock made me and Gypsy jump. *Who the hell is it now?* I stomped over to the door and whipped it open to find Jackson casually leaning against the door frame... again.

"You ready?" he asked.

"That hour didn't feel very long." I noted.

"I decided to speed things up. Your training clothes should be in the dresser. Meet me downstairs." Without another word, Jackson disappeared down the staircase.

I sighed deeply and shut the door. I walked over to my dresser and started to rummage through the clothes, trying to find anything that looked like 'training clothes'.

"Here, let me help," offered Gypsy.

I stepped aside as Gypsy found a pair of workout pants and a t-shirt. "If I'm correct, Jackson will have a pair of sneakers for you downstairs." She handed me the outfit before heading for the door. "Good luck! We'll talk later!" She waved goodbye before leaving me alone to change.

I ripped off my clothes and threw on the workout pants and black t-shirt. *Shit, I forgot to ask Gypsy about the bathroom,* I thought. I ran my fingers through my hair and adjusted myself one more time before I headed downstairs to see Grumpy Pants. Just like Gypsy had said, Jackson held a pair of black Nike shoes and a sour look on his beautiful face. *Fuck me.* Jackson tossed me the pair and walked out the door. I untied the shoes and slipped them on before running after him. Jackson grabbed my arm once I was out the door and dragged me to a path behind the house.

"Hey, what is your deal?" I asked frustrated.

"No time to waste, kiddo, we must get to work *now*," snapped Jackson. His movements were rushed, and I couldn't understand his sudden urgency.

I huffed internally before we made it to the end of the path behind the house. We approached the deep, green backyard that I'd seen from my window in my room. The moon was so bright, it lit up the whole backyard and made every shadow dance before us. Each tree swayed peacefully with whatever leaves they had left on them. All the open space before us was breathtaking. Cool air pinched my cheeks, but with my new self, I could tolerate it. In the middle of the yard was a giant white blanket and two black pillows seated across each other. Fog lights guided our way as Jackson led me over to the center before letting go of my arm and directed me to sit on one of the black pillows. I sat crossed-legged with Jackson and waited for his instructions.

"First lesson is to teach you to focus. I need your full attention," said Jackson.

"I thought you were teaching me how to fight?"

He sighed heavily. "Yes, but there are steps to take before we get to the fighting. You can't throw yourself in battle without understanding your new strength."

Autumn air tickled my skin, and being under Jacksons' stare was no help when it came to focusing either. "Okay. I'm ready."

"I just want you to close your eyes and empty your mind of any negativity. Breathe in and out deeply as you release that energy," instructed Jackson. "I need my trainee to have a clear mind from boy problems."

Our eyes locked as I began to piece together that he must had overheard Gypsy and I's conversation. The real question was; how much. "It's rude to snoop on someone else's *private* conversation."

"It's not so private if said girls are being loud about it. Now, do as I say."

I swallowed back a snarky comment and began to breathe in and out with my eyes closed. I let go of all the confusion and uneasiness of the past day and let it all go, especially Jackson's eavesdropping. After what seemed like a good five minutes of excessive breathing, Jackson snapped his fingers together to have me focus back on him.

"How do you feel?" he asked.

"Relaxed," I answered. The energy around us seemed content, for now.

"Good, now stand up and step away from the blanket," he ordered.

I did as he said and waited. I watched Jackson fold the blanket and toss the pillows to the side. He circled me a few times before he stood behind me. My heart kicked a few notches forward from how close he was to me.

"Close your eyes again and picture yourself standing in the middle of a battle zone. Your enemies are everywhere. See how they move and attack. Watch their steps and defense," he whispered behind me.

I closed my eyes once again and pictured exactly what Jackson described. I stood in fire and chaos. Buildings were crumbled, and trees were burned. I pictured my enemies, whoever they were, as knights fighting for their kingdom. Swords swooshed in different directions, and shields clashed against them. I analyzed my fake battle zone, surprised that I'd come up with such detail so quickly. One of the knights removed his helmet to reveal a pretty set of fangs and latched on someone's neck. Blood overflowed, spraying everywhere. I could feel Jackson's presence hover closer to me, which caused the hair on my arms to stand up.

"Watch as they take down your comrades. Watch the blood paint the ground crimson. Feel the anger and adrenaline from wanting to hurt those who killed your loved ones," said Jackson.

The anger inside me grew as each member of my team was slaughtered in plain sight. Body parts were ripped to shreds, scattered throughout the gruesome battlefield. I balled my fist up and waited for my turn.

A soft hand grazed my right arm that sent chills and my heart rate to another level. "Do you feel it?" Jackson's voiced whispered against my ear. He gently moved his hand down my arm, giving me that same passionate feeling we shared in my room before. His other hand reached around to grip my wrist tenderly, clouding my battle zone daydream. *Focus, Ivy!* I thought. I stood completely still, afraid to even move an inch.

"Your enemies are dying to taste you," Jackson said while he placed his smooth mouth on my neck.

Before I could react to his touch, his soft kiss to my neck, the way he held me tenderly, he grabbed me tighter and flipped me over on my back. I groaned when I hit the ground and rubbed my head from the slight pressure.

"Always watch your back, little dhampir," he snorted before leaving me on the cold hard ground.

CHAPTER 8

"What the fuck was that?" I snapped while I got myself up off the ground.

Jackson turned around with a sly smirk on his pretty face. "The first rule of being a dhampir or a vampire is don't be so easily influenced by emotions."

"And what emotion was that?" I asked.

"Passion. You got distracted because I gave you that," he said.

"Are you telling me not to feel when I'm in battle?"

"Precisely."

"That's a load of shit. Anger was my emotion."

"Obviously not. Your body language gave you away too easily."

I wiped the dirt off my butt and stomped over to him, getting in his face. "Is that what you do to all the trainees? Kiss their necks?"

Jackson grimaced and got even closer to my face. "Don't think you're so special."

Anger boiled in my blood. I acted quickly, grabbing ahold of Jackson's arm and twisting it before I knocked him to the ground.

"How about now?" I said. I twisted it harder, making sure he felt every inch of pain from my hold.

Jackson pushed against my hold, but I had the perfect position to keep him locked. He struggled for a few moments before slumping down into the grass. "Okay, you made your point."

I smiled, but as soon as I let go, Jackson kicked my legs out from under me and knocked me back on my ass. He stood up, laughing and shaking the grass out of his soft, blond hair.

"You're stronger than I thought, but not as quick as me," he chuckled.

I rolled my eyes as I got up again and wiped another patch of dirt off my bum. Without thinking, I sprinted forward and tackled Jackson to the ground, getting a mouth full of grass on my way down. Jackson tossed me to the side, knocking the wind out of me. He got up and staggered forward, trying to escape. I rushed up and hopped on his back, dragging him once again down with me. We rolled around on the grass until I was underneath him, my breathing hard. Jackson's gray eyes stared deep into mine. He reached for my face and tucked a loose strand of hair behind my ear, making my heart thump erratically in my ribcage. I watched his eyes focus on my mouth as he began to trace it with his finger. His lips parted, making me think he was about to kiss me. *Oh my God is he?* I thought. *This is wrong.* But my heart said something different.

"Not bad," he whispered.

Without a word, Jackson lifted himself up and walked over to the folded blanket and pillows. I lay there, feeling rejection and embarrassment color my face. I decided not to mention our little moment again and got up to meet him at the blanket. He handed it to me while he snatched the pillows and headed straight back to the house.

"I wanted to ease you into our training. I don't mess around. I need you to focus," said Jackson.

I chewed the inside of my cheek and kept my eyes ahead. I knew he was right, but why would he toy with me like that? He'd kissed my neck and made it seem completely normal, and I was convinced he had totally forgotten about our little encounter in my room earlier. Was he actually training me? Or was he messing with my head? We found the trail that led around to the front of the house and walked the rest of the way in silence.

That's when I smelled it. The sweet, dangerously thick smell that had me watering at the mouth and filled my lungs with pain. Jackson could sense it too and rushed forward to the front of the house without hesitation. I followed as fast as I could, when Jackson came to an erupt stop at the foot of the steps. I moved around him to find something that took my breath away. A young girl in a white dress was sprawled out on the steps, soaked in her own blood. Her dark hair fanned out on the top step, while her legs occupied the bottom. My slow heart skipped a beat when I saw the blood pool on the last step. I swallowed the hunger and watched Jackson pull a cellphone out of his pocket and dial quickly. I turned my attention back to the girl and saw lacerations on her arms and legs. Her face was bruised, and blood dripped from her scalp. The hunger grew, and I wanted so badly to stick my fingers in the pool of blood, but this was not the time or place to become an addict.

"Theodore," Jackson said into the phone.

I walked a bit closer to observe the mysterious young girl. *Who did this to her?* I thought. *And why leave the body here?*

"It happened again. This time, the victim is dead," whispered Jackson.

I staggered back from the dead girl's body and looked at Jackson with worry on my face. *This has happened before?* A small breeze swept around me, wafting the smell into my nose and filling my mind with dangerous thoughts. I tried to breathe in and out, but the hunger took over, and I was already kneeling down with my hands in a pool of blood before I heard Jackson drop his phone.

"IVY! STOP!" Jackson shouted while he pulled me back.

I ended up against the side of the house with Jackson's hands pinned at my shoulders. The blood was still on my fingers, but I couldn't move my arms to bring it to my mouth. An owl, hooted not far from where we stood. Leaves rolled at our feet as the wind picked up, and the moon disappeared behind a tall oak.

"Ivy, look at me," ordered Jackson.

I closed my eyes and ignored his demand, wanting so badly to taste my fingers.

"IVY! LOOK AT ME, DAMMIT!" he shouted.

I flinched and creaked my eyes open to see Jackson's worried expression spread across his face.

"You need to control it. You have to," he said.

I swallowed another hungry feeling and leaned my head against the brick siding. The pain in my throat, the tingle in my mouth, the desire in my stomach was yelling at me to taste, but my mind was fighting between what was good and bad. Jackson kept me pinned to the wall while he wiped my fingers with the edge his shirt.

"I believe our next lesson is to control our hunger," suggested Jackson.

The smell disappeared, but the tingle in my mouth lingered. "I'm sorry."

Jackson finally unpinned me and stepped back. "It's fine, but I need to get you out of here. The Vamps need to take care of this."

I nodded and let Jackson lead the way back around the house. "We'll take the back door. To avoid questions."

I took one last glance behind me at the poor dead girl and shuddered when I remembered sticking my hand in her blood. *I'm a fucking freak,* I thought.

We finally reached the back door, and Jackson hurried us inside. We ended up near one of the side rooms off the foyer. It had a few end tables and some black couches neatly placed in the corner. A giant window cast the night shadows from the moon on the hard, wooden floors, and there were two bookcases that were placed on the opposite side of the window. Jackson opened the door in front of the room, and we were right where I'd first entered the house.

"Go take a shower and avoid everyone," he instructed.

"What about you?" I asked. My mind was still spinning from the blood. I was so close to tasting it.

"I'm going to speak with Theodore and make sure everything is clear," he said.

Jackson nudged me to the stairs and disappeared back out the side door we'd just come from. I ran up the stairs and smacked right into what felt like a hard boulder. Rebecca.

"Watch where you're going, dumbass," she snapped.

"Sorry, my bad," I said quickly.

"Where's Jackson?" asked Rebecca. Still wearing her slutty pajamas, she rubbed her eyes to get a better look at me.

"I don't know," I lied.

She eyed me up and down before getting in my face. "You don't know?"

"No."

Rebecca cackled and pushed past me. "Later, dork."

What a fucking bitch, I thought. I finally made it to my room and shut the door behind me. Instead of doing what Jackson ordered, I slid down against the door and covered my face with my hands, sobbing uncontrollably. *What is going on here?*

CHAPTER 9

I rubbed my eyes after a good long cry and lifted myself up from the ground. My eyes were sore, and my throat was dry from all the pathetic crying I'd done. Everything was piling on my shoulders, and I was afraid of collapsing under all this mess. Completely unaware of what came over me, I stood there, aimlessly trying to figure out what to do next. Do I follow Jackson's orders? Or do I find him? It was a back and forth battle in my head, until I finally decided against my better judgement and went to look for Jackson. I couldn't sit there any longer and couldn't pretend that I hadn't seen a dead girl laying sprawled out on the front steps.

I brushed the mess out of my hair and wiped the last few tears from my eyes before heading back out to the hallway. *Now, where do I find him?* I thought. *Maybe if I ask Gypsy?* But I didn't want to bring her into this mess, especially since Jackson had ordered me to avoid everyone. I decided to start downstairs and go to the other side of the building. I rushed down the stairs as quietly as I could and tried the second door to the right from where Jackson and I had come through earlier. I opened it to find a dimly-lit, long hallway covered in maroon wallpaper. The rug was a rustic brown and candles separated portraits of people I didn't know. Trusting my gut, I made my way down the hall to the last door. This door felt different than the rest. This door could hold some missing holes of my visions. I swallowed hard and reached for the doorknob, turning it slowly. It revealed another set of rooms down another small hallway. *My god, this place is a maze,* I thought. It was the voice at the end of the hall that wiped the disappointment from my thoughts.

"You don't understand... she can't know!" someone shouted.

"And she won't. If we have to, we'll wipe her memory," said another.

"No. I will not have you ruin this girl... again," said a familiar voice. Theodore? Theodore!

"Theodore, you fail to see the downfall of this situation. She wasn't supposed to know any of this. Now, we have to find some tall tale to tell this girl. It's blasphemy!"

I scooted closer to the door, noticing it was ajar. Peeking inside, I could see unfamiliar faces surrounding a long wooden table. A man with long silver hair grazed his white, silky chin with a long finger, almost like he was contemplating something.

Finally, after what seemed like a million years, the silver haired man stood from his chair. "I will not have this girl ruin what we have. She must be compelled to forget."

"NO!" shouted another familiar voice.

"Jackson, please," begged Theodore. My heart ached when I heard his name.

"You will not speak to us this way, Jackson. You're a dhampir. Remember your place," said a stern female voice.

The air around me became thick with anxiety as time passed on. I knew this was about me, but I just didn't understand what the big deal was? Why couldn't I know?

"We should ask the young lady how she feels about this," said a soft voice.

"We don't have to. She's outside the door as we speak."

My heart stopped, and I stepped back from the threshold, ready to run. The door whipped open to reveal Jackson's stone-cold stare. He lifted his hand to gesture me inside, but from the look on his face, I could tell he hoped I wouldn't come in. I gulped down the anxiety and walked inside the dimly lit room, ready to face the crowd of angry Vamps.

A long, dark, wooden table covered more of the room than the Vamps who surrounded it. At least eight of them, including Theodore and Aurora, were seated around it. There, sitting like statues around the table, were seven other pairs of judging eyes grilling into me. All dressed in dark clothing, their striking features intimidated me to the point where I stood frozen at the entrance, afraid to take a step forward. Jackson came up behind me and grabbed my forearm, leading me toward the table. I acted without hesitation as fear sliced through my core. I could sense they were older, much older than Jackson, but their presence terrified me. These Vamps had wisdom and power, and from what I could sense, their power was more than Theodore could ever have. Jackson led me to a seat right across from Theodore's, which I assumed was Jackson's, as he stood behind me and rested his hands on the back of the chair. I looked around and studied the other Vamps closer. Still petrified, I looked at them head on, trying to hide my fear. The three gentlemen up front told the others they were top dog. The one in the middle with the silver hair eyed me before sitting back down in his seat.

"Ivy," he said.

I stared into his cool blue eyes, afraid to even speak. Gazing around, unsure, I noticed three other females and another male sat on either side of the head Vamps.

"You can call me Artimis, and this," he gestured toward the two men beside him, "is Calix, and Sebastian." Calix had black hair that touched his shoulders and made his pale skin shine in the light. He had soft brown eyes and a pointy nose. He nodded politely to me. Sebastian was an auburn-haired beauty with hazel eyes that glistened when he smiled at me. Surprised by this, I slightly smiled in return.

Artimis moved from his spot at the head of the table and walked over to the opposite side from where I sat to place himself behind a beautiful brunette with silver streaks in her hair. "Juliet." Her deep, green eyes narrowed in on me like I was a mouse caught in a snake pit. I shifted uncomfortably in my chair and tried unsuccessfully to avoid her stare. She captivated my attention in a hostile way. Artimis moved down the line to another male with jet black hair, but his eyes were a soft gray, and he had a giant scar on his left cheek. "Finn." Artimis strode back to the front, avoiding Aurora and Theodore's eyes, and introduced the last two ladies at the table. "Noella and Honor." Noella was a pretty, petite thing with violet hair and turquoise eyes. Honor was a soft blonde and had a round face that looked almost childlike. Honor was the first person that I'd ever seen where one eye was blue and the other was brown. It fascinated me, and I couldn't stop staring. She smiled at me but turned her attention back to Artimis as he took his place back at the head of the table. From the structure of them, this was indeed the Imperium Council. Dressed in the blackest black, they looked like they were attending a funeral. My funeral.

"We're the Imperium Council. For centuries, this council has maintained control of the northeast side of America. Do you know what Imperium stands for, Ivy?" asked Artimis.

When I didn't say anything, he smiled like a Cheshire cat.

"Absolute power. We're the stronger fraction of our vampire race. And if anyone decides that we don't belong, well, then, we take care of it." The threat was loud and clear and made the hairs on my arms stand.

"Now that introductions are complete, we must discuss the real issue at hand," announced Artimis.

All nine pairs of eyes grilled into me from different positions of the room. I could feel the anxiety creep back up into my lungs, making it harder to breathe.

"She's the only dhampir who knows. It's not a big deal," said Jackson.

"Silence, half breed. You're lucky we let you be a part of this council to begin with," snapped Finn.

Jackson gripped the back of the chair I sat on. The action vibrated the chair, which made me more uneasy than before. I wanted so badly to comfort him, but it would be weird, and I shouldn't because he also treated me like shit. *I'm an idiot*, I thought.

"She must be compelled. It is the only way," said the vampire named Calix.

"Why? She only saw a dead body, that's it. I don't see the issue," defended Noella.

"Noella, how can you still be naïve?" laughed Juliet.

"I'm not. So take the thorn out of your side, Juliet," retaliated Noella.

A tingle in my throat began to form, which caused me to lose focus on the conversation. The last time I'd fed was before the training with Jackson, but it wasn't that long ago. *How could I be craving more now?* I thought. My head felt heavy, like a thirty-pound weight had been sitting atop it for the past hour. I tried to focus on the conversation, but the hunger was rising, and my patience started to falter.

"How can we trust this young dhampir?" asked Honor.

"We can't," retorted Juliet. *I really hate this bitch*, I thought.

"Fuck off, Juliet," said Jackson. His hands shook my seat even more than before.

"Jackson, silence," commanded Theodore.

"I think we should vote," said Calix.

Simultaneously, everyone, including myself, turned our attention to Calix. The room was silenced for what seemed like years. The early morning birds stopped chirping outside, and the slight breeze that rustled the trees came to a halt. Calix rose from his seat, showing off a long, deep, purple robe that wrapped around his slender body.

"Since we all can't come to a civil agreement, we will vote," he said.

"When?" asked Juliet.

"Before dawn," Calix responded.

"That is fair. It would give us time to mull things over," mumbled Sebastian.

"Only the *vampires* will vote, though," Juliet said as she gave Jackson a dirty glare.

"Yes, of course," replied Artimis as he leaned back in his chair.

I looked over at Theodore and Aurora, wanting to see their reaction. Not one of them held any emotion. I was flabbergasted.

"We will come back here just before dawn. Is that agreeable?" asked Calix.

"Yes," they all agreed.

My thoughts and feelings boiled over, so I stood up, knocked Jackson back against the wall, and stormed out of the room. Even though they were done, I wasn't going to sit there any longer and be picked apart because of something that wasn't my fault. They already took my memories before by changing me, I was not going to go through it again. I could run away? Maybe I could handle this dhampir life on my own? I darted down the hall, trying to escape as quickly as I could. Out of the corner of my eye, Jackson caught up to me and tackled me down on the floor. We rolled over a few times before he had been pinned under him, both of my arms pushed down.

"Let me go!" I shouted.

"Ivy, you're starving and mad. Do not leave," he said.

"I don't give a shit! NOW, LET ME GO!" I screamed. I wiggled under him and tried to break free, but he was right. My hunger got the best of me, and it made me weak under his hold. A sudden rush of hunger came over me, tightened my lungs, desperate to taste blood. Human blood.

"Ivy, we need to talk, but not here," whispered Jackson.

"Okay," I mumbled. Something wasn't right. This whole situation wasn't right.

"Go shower, and I'll get you some blood, okay? And this time, listen to me," he said.

Jackson released his hold on me and helped me to my feet. I brushed myself off and looked at him. His soft gray eyes held a secret that I would soon find out, and that scared me. Was I ready for the truth? Definitely not, but I didn't want my memories taken again.

"I'll come to you when I'm ready," said Jackson.

Without another word, we parted ways.

CHAPTER 10

After four failed attempts of trying to find the bathroom, I finally came across it at the very end of the hallway. Granted, the big "women's" sign on the door was a dead giveaway, but I managed without having to wake up the whole mansion. The bathroom was wide and consisted of four rows of showers and a long countertop with four sinks. A long mirror spread out on the wall above the sinks, and navy-blue hand towels were displayed neatly on the opposite side. White tiles were contrasted beautifully with gray walls. I undressed and stepped into one of the clean showers, basking in the hot water that trickled down my skin. Inside, the shower contained a variety of shampoos and soaps. I picked the pretty pink bottle of shampoo and rubbed the thick liquid in my hair. After I rinsed out the shampoo, I grabbed the conditioner and had it settle in my scalp. Soaked from head to toe, I leaned my forehead against the shower wall and breathed deeply in and out through my nose. It had been a while since I'd found peace and quiet.

My thoughts rattled against my brain as I tried to control them in order. First, I saw a dead body. Second, I found myself in front of the whole Imperium Council. The way Artimis spoke about the council gave me an unpleasant feeling. Third, they're voting for me to have my memory wiped. And last, but not least, Jackson had a secret to tell me, and at this point, I just wanted to be dead. So many secrets in this place. And I still can't control my bloodlust.

My bloodlust. It felt so good. I wanted it all the time. I leaned my head back into the water and rinsed out the conditioner. I wanted so badly to feed from that dead girl. A dead girl! How fucked up is that? But that was just a dead girl. I imagined fresh blood from a human's vein as it pulsates under the skin would be heavenly. I needed dhampir therapy.

On top of that, Jackson was mind fucking me with his emotions. I won't lie, there was something there. *No, Ivy. There* is, I thought. He made me feel so mad at times, yet so breathless at others. I knew he was taken, but I felt like he knew something more about me than what he was letting on to. I was so conflicted with my feelings, and yet I couldn't help to be pulled by his touch. Not only was it a bad idea to even think about Jackson in that way, I would have Rebecca at my neck in two seconds if she found out.

I finished up in the shower and stepped out, wrapping myself in a thick gray towel. I walked over to the mirror and wiped away the fog. My face looked flushed, but my eyes told a different story. I was exhausted mentally, and I had no idea how I was still standing on my own two feet. My throat throbbed from hunger, and I wanted so badly to drain someone. Such an inner turmoil within myself.

I dried myself off and threw on a new pair of black sweats, a jumbo, gray sweatshirt, slipped on a fresh pair of white socks, and shook the rest of my wet hair in my towel. Of course, there was no hamper to be found, so I decided to lug it back with me to my room. The walk back was treacherous because I knew I would have to face Jackson and the pending doom of my memory on the line. It wasn't fair, and I was tired of not remembering who I was. I stopped outside my bedroom door and hesitated at the doorknob. I hadn't had a vision in such a long time, and I was aching to know if it would ever come back. I had no idea how to trigger them. The visions held some type of truth or message that could be the key to my past. That was the one theory I had that made the most sense.

I turned the doorknob and saw Jackson's body spread out on my bed. He'd changed his clothes, this time, he was wearing jeans and a plaid shirt where he left a few buttons undone to expose his chest. My heart hammered like a woodpecker until he looked up from his phone and frowned.

"What?" I snapped.

"You know there's a hamper in the laundry room, right?" he said.

I clenched my dirty clothes and towels before throwing them at his face. "Take care of it, then." I wasn't even going to mention I had no idea where the laundry room was. Maybe Gypsy could give me an actual grand tour. If I remembered.

Jackson tossed them on the floor before he rummaged through his pockets to pull out another vial of blood. My mouth began to water as I stepped forward to retrieve my dinner. I reached for it, ready to devour the deliciousness when suddenly, Jackson held it from my reach.

"Ivy," he said.

My heart stuttered when he said my name. His eyes portrayed a deep sadness that even I couldn't even begin to understand. I continued to be silent and waited for him to start again.

"I just want you to know that whatever happens, I'm sorry I couldn't protect you," he confessed.

My mouth went dry. I looked awkwardly away, not sure how to respond.

"Anyway, here's your dinner," Jackson said as he tossed the vial directly at my forehead.

"Wow, and here I thought you were being nice for once," I said as I picked up the vial off the floor. *God, he's bipolar*, I thought.

"I try," he laughed.

I ignored his comment and proceeded to drain the contents of the vial. The rush consumed me, and I was left once again high and needy for more like a kid in a candy store. I walked over to the window and leaned forward on the windowsill. *Maybe if I ignore him long enough, he will go away*, I thought. Jackson shifted behind me on the bed, I continued to ignore him.

"Ivy," he said again in that soft tone.

"What, Jackson? Do you want something?" I asked.

"The Imperium Council are ruthless. They will do anything to protect their precious coven. What you saw in there is the exact reason why we are the way we are," said Jackson.

"Yeah, I saw," I grumbled.

"I'm hoping some vote against you being compelled. Because what I want...."

"What is that?" I interrupted. I turned around and faced him finally. His expression was lifted into a crooked smile.

"What is what?" he asked. Completely amused by my sudden anger.

"Compelled?"

"A full-blooded vampire can compel a human's, even a dhampir's, mind to make them forget things. How it's done... it can be... frightening."

"Honestly, what else are you guys not telling me. I feel like I'm being held accountable for information about this vampire shit, and I'm sick of it!" I yelled.

Jackson jumped up from my bed and closed the distance between us. He placed his hands on my shoulders so he could keep me focused on him. His gray eyes had me captivated and a little breathless. He made me feel on fire, and yet at the same time, cold as a bucket of ice. *Why do I feel this way?* I thought. *Why?*

"I can tell you anything you want to know, but I need to tell you something first. I can't even trust Rebecca with this," said Jackson.

"Me? Don't you hate me?" I laughed.

"I don't hate you. I just don't have patience for a baby dhampir, but that's beside the point. The Imperium Council is hiding something about those bodies. This wasn't the first one."

"Yeah, I heard that earlier when you were on the phone," I stated.

"Well, there was one two weeks before your arrival and two other ones a couple months back. At first, we thought it was a bunch of dhampirs fucking with us, but then I snuck into the basement where Theodore and the rest of the Vamps keep their personal blood donations, and I discovered they'd kept the girls' dead bodies," explained Jackson.

"So, they kept drained bodies in the basement? For what? To hide the evidence?" I questioned.

"That's just it. Evidence. I checked out the bodies and saw on their necks a symbol. Almost like a personal stamp..." he trailed off as he stepped back from me. I watched Jackson pace the room. He looked confused as he looked around where he stood, "Paper, I need paper and a pen to show you," he finally said.

"Umm I don't think I have any of that here," I said.

Jackson left the room with rushed footsteps echoing down the hall. I could hear him rummaging in a room in the distance, opening and closing drawers as they slammed back into place. He came back with a black notebook and a pen, flipped it opened on top of my dresser, and began to draw the symbol.

"Here," he said as he handed me the notebook.

From what I could comprehend, it was shaped as half a heart that seemed to break off at the end, turned into a slight teardrop then looped back up to cross through the half heart. It was an interesting symbol, a symbol I had no idea what it meant, but if this was on the dead girl's bodies like Jackson said, then my gut knew this wasn't good. I traced the pattern with my finger, memorizing the style until it was engraved in my brain.

"This isn't some stamp, it's a warning," I whispered.

"What?" Jackson jumped.

"Jackson, this is a warning. A threat. That's what I feel when I look at this. You said this has been happening for a couple months, right? Only females? It's a threat, and there's a reason they're only using females to send the message," I explained. My gut throbbed when I came to the realization of this. I knew I was right. There was something else Jackson said about the body and I couldn't remember what exactly, but the thought sat at the tip of my tongue.

Jackson ran his long fingers through his untucked hair, glancing back down at the notebook. "A warning," he repeated.

"What kind of warning?" a familiar voice said behind us.

My whole body froze as Jackson's eyes met mine with the same fear. A caramel hand reached out and took the notebook from my grasp. I followed the hand to reveal Gypsy, smiling from ear to ear.

"What the fuck, Gypsy!" yelled Jackson.

"You should've seen your face! Awesome, right? I love doing voice impressions. Theodore is too easy to master," she giggled.

"How are you awake right now?" he asked.

"Hmm let's see," Gypsy said as she dangled the notebook from her fingers. "Dhampir rule number one, Jackson. You need to be quiet when you're trying to be sneaky. Also, for someone who is a dhampir, you're incredibly loud."

"Gypsy," I said.

"Ivy, it's okay. I won't tell anyone," she promised.

"How do we even know? How can we be sure you won't go running to tell the whole council?" Jackson questioned.

If looks could kill, I swear Gypsy would've ended Jackson in a second. I watched her walk over to him, grip his t-shirt with her hand, and yank him forward to her eye level.

"Listen here, punk. I'm the *only* one you can trust in this goddamn place. And I'm the last person you should question about loyalty," snapped Gypsy.

Jackson's face flared a crimson red before stepping back from Gypsy's grasp. He fixed the front of his shirt, and without another glance in my direction, he stormed out of my room, slamming the door behind him. Unfazed by Jackson's sudden departure, Gypsy sat back down on my bed and stared at the symbol in the notebook. I stood in place, confused by what Gypsy had said, stunned by how Jackson had reacted. It was never black and white with him, it was always a ray of colors. Always complicated.

"Gypsy... what was that about?" I asked.

"Jackson being a twit, that's all," she mumbled.

Deciding not to press it further, I shook off the negative reaction from Jackson and joined Gypsy on the bed. I watched her trace her own finger over the image.

She then flipped the notebook in different directions, looking at it from all sides.

"I'm guessing you heard everything," I assumed as I watched her examine the symbol.

"Yes," she continued to twist the notebook around, "interesting," she murmured as she retraced her pointer finger on the symbol.

"Have you seen this before?" I asked.

"I think so. This mansion has a library you know. I sometimes go there and read of our history. There isn't much on it, but I've done some snooping, and I found a little section of books in the top corner of the library that is restricted to us. This symbol might be in one of them," she said.

"How do we get it?"

"I need to get the key from one of the Imperium Council members. And by need—I mean steal."

"Oh boy."

Gypsy threw her head back and laughed. "This will be a piece of cake!"

She jumped up from my bed and handed me back the notebook then smoothed down her pajama pants and headed toward the door.

"Gypsy!" I called.

"Girl, don't worry and relax for a bit. I heard about what happened earlier. Let me handle the rest," she said before disappearing into her room.

I huffed a heavy sigh before getting up to close my bedroom door. *Great. What more can be added to my plate?* I thought as I gathered the heavy curtains together to shut out the bright moon, even though it was comforting, pulled back the comforter to my bed, crawled under the covers, and stared up at my plain, white ceiling. I trusted Gypsy. Her intentions were good, and I knew I'd always have her in my corner. Jackson... Jackson had me feeling he knew more than what he was letting on. One minute he was smoldering like a piece of coal, the next he was as frigid as an ice storm. What was worse was this Imperium Council I was ruled under literally wanted my memories fried. So many secrets in one place, and yet I felt like I was lost in a maze with them.

I rolled over to check my alarm clock. It was two a.m. I groaned. I couldn't follow this new sleeping schedule to save my life. Then again, I had no clue of what my sleeping schedule was like before all of this. The memory was all I had of my past life. The more I replay it in my head, the more certain I am it was me, and I wanted to tell Jackson about all of this, but the way he acted pushed me further away from telling him the truth. For now, Gypsy was all I had in this crazy mess. Theodore, however, had been distant as ever with me. For someone who was my mentor, he really seemed to bring his distance and lack of guidance to a whole new level. Ironic how Jackson became both in less than a day. Theodore was another person with a hidden agenda. I was not in the mood to be played twice by two people who claimed they cared about me. I would have to get the bottom of this myself. And fast.

What would be the harm in taking a nap? I thought. Exhaustion crept in like a serial killer, attacking me from out of nowhere. Soon, I was knocked out, floating in a cloud formation above the sky.

I was running through a thickly fogged forest, my footsteps echoed with every step I took. My hair whipped around me as I pushed myself forward as fast as I could. The hair on my arms rose as I could sense I was being followed. Fear ran through my veins, making me on edge as I continued down the path of an unknown destination. I could hear another pair of feet following closely behind me. I picked up the pace as the forest path wound around a bunch of hollow trees. I knew I needed to get to the end, and fast. Something was not right with this dream. I felt exposed, even within the fog. Eventually, the path widened and showed a small cabin perched perfectly on top of a hill. An iron gate was wrapped around the perimeter of the property, and I knew in my gut I needed to get inside. I reached the gate and realized it was rusted shut. I hopped over the fence, and my leg got caught on one of the iron pegs. I tugged hard and felt the peg rip my jeans, stabbing my shin. I groaned and limped up the hill to the cabin. The footsteps behind me disappeared as I reached the front door. I jiggled the knob, expecting it to be locked. With luck, it turned, and I stumbled inside into a warm, cozy cabin. The air inside smelled of pinecones and peppermint. I closed the door behind me and trekked over to the cabinets in the kitchen, trying to find any resemblance of a first aid kit. That's when I heard the scream below me.

I jumped. My heart pounded heavily inside my rib cage. My mind said run away, but my gut said I needed to investigate. I slowly rounded the corner away from the kitchen and headed toward the back of the cabin. A door was propped open by a wooden chair, casting a haunting light through the entryway. This wasn't safe, I knew it, but I needed to know what was down there. I swallowed the fear that was rising in my lungs, quietly opened the door, and descended downstairs. The eerie light I'd seen from upstairs was coming from the back corner of the basement. The floor was cement, and there were shelves upon shelves of junk and dust all piled together. Another scream bounced off the stone walls. I covered my ears, trying to block out the chilling sound. I knew I was getting closer. The shelves seemed to narrow the farther I got down the line. I rounded the corner where the light was casting on a girl with long dark hair huddled in the corner. Blood was pooling at her feet as she whimpered softly to herself.

"Are you okay?" I asked.

She froze. She lifted her head to show me her big brown eyes. Fear and confusion covered her face along with a deep gash across her cheek.

"You better leave. He will come for you too," she warned.

"Who?" I asked.

The front door to the cabin slammed shut. The girl turned back to face the corner.

"I need to get you out of here," I said.

"It's too late. I've been branded," she whimpered.

"Wha...?" Footsteps began to trek slowly down the basement stairs.

The girl moved her hair from the back of her neck to reveal a mark. A mark so familiar it had my throat tighten in fear.

"Now go!" she whispered.

The heavy footsteps stopped abruptly at the other end of the basement. My heart was hammering so loud, the animals outside could hear it. One last look down at the girl who was staring back at me with those scared eyes gave me the power to move my feet. I ducked behind another row of shelves and heard the footsteps pick up again. I watched in horror as a tall figure emerged in front of the girl. The figure wore a black trench coat and a baseball cap to hide their face.

"Who were you talking to?" he asked.

"No one," she said.

A loud smack echoed off the walls as the girl fell forward, crying in pain.

"Lie to me again and your death will be sooner rather than later," he warned.

I gulped and stepped backward, wanting to exit myself quickly from this nightmare, when my foot got caught on a box, and I tumbled backward into the mess. I watched as the mystery man in the trench coat and baseball cap turn in my direction. Without hesitation, he ran toward me, a gun raised in my direction. I scrambled to my feet and booked it down another isle of junk.

"Come out, come out wherever you are," the man teased.

He was closing in on me, and I needed to think fast. I looked around for a window when I noticed it was right above the girl on the floor. Great. I had to create some kind of diversion. That was the only way to get the hell out of there. I rounded another corner of junk filled shelves, and without thinking, I pushed them to the ground. Bottles escaped from the top, smashing to the floor.

"There you are," he laughed.

I dashed around the other side of the shelf and ran full speed to the window. The girl on the floor stood in my way, an evil smile on her face.

"You're too late," she cackled.

Her eyes were now glowing a deep red, while her face had dark veins illuminated on her pale complexion.

Panic rose in my chest when I felt the man in the trench coat behind me. I turned around to the gun pointed at my temple. It felt cold against my clammy forehead. His cap covered his eyes, but the smile plastered on his lips made me cringe.

"Now I have you right where I want you, pretty," he mused.

The trigger to the gun clicked and I closed my eyes, bracing for the impact of the bullet.

CHAPTER 11

"Ivy! Wake up!"

The voice didn't sound familiar at first. I felt strong hands on my shoulders, and the smell of minty breath fanned my face. My mind seemed slower than my reaction to the person shaking me. I felt locked in my sleep, unable to escape. Was the man in my dream here with me now? Was he coming to finish the job? Terror rang true through my bones as I thrashed at the person who was gripping me so tightly.

"Stop! Let me go!" I shouted.

"Ivy!"

"No!"

"Ivy, goddammit snap out of it!"

The fog in my head seemed to disperse when the voice shouted back at me. I jerked awake to find Jackson shaking my shoulders violently. He leaned over me with deep concern in those gray eyes. Sweat poured down my face from my hairline as I tried to recollect what happened in my dream. Jackson brushed my hair away from my face along with my sweat. I was relieved it wasn't the man in the trench coat, but terrified that he might actually be real.

"Are you alright?" he asked.

I pushed myself up against my pillow, resting my head on the wall behind me. My breathing came in ragged spurts. My head pounded harder than a set of drums.

"Yeah... yeah, I'm okay," I mumbled. Was I? The dream echoed in my mind. The man in the trench coat, the girl with the dark red eyes... the mark... that mark.

"Ivy, I came to tell you I won't be allowed in the room for the verdict," he said, interrupting my thoughts.

"Wait what?" I sat up, which caused my head to spin a bit.

Jackson sighed and scratched his arm in a nonchalant manner, "Yeah."

"They're going to chew me apart..."

"No. No, I'm going to prepare you before you walk in there. Give you some insight on all the members."

"How? It isn't going to change anything. You saw how quickly they wanted me to forget. They were ready to throw me to the wolves!"

"Not all of them."

I rubbed my temples, trying to concentrate on the conversation. The nightmare lingered at the back of my mind. I couldn't deal with this all at once. Covering my hands with my face, I sighed deeply in frustration. Big hands stroked my hair, and I knew Jackson was trying to comfort me, but my inner thoughts nagged inside my head, reminding me this might be the end.

"I can't do this anymore," I finally said.

"Ivy," mused Jackson. His hands tugged at my arms, pulling them away from my face. He looked at me like he was seeing the sun for the first time. My heart stammered in response to his intense stare. *You're so handsome*, I thought. Never letting go from me, Jackson started to lean in. My mind raced as my body followed in pursuit. His lips, those full lips, inches from my own, brushed against mine slightly, when a cell phone went off. We both jerked away, afraid we'd been caught in the act. Jackson reached for his phone in his pocket and answered on the second ring.

"Yeah?"

A muffled voice vibrated through his phone's speaker.

"Rebecca, I can't right now."

I mentally rolled my eyes at the mention of her name. Even if Jackson didn't have this effect on me, she was still a bitch for no reason. Then again, I shouldn't even be all over him. As much as I couldn't stand her, if that was my boyfriend trying to mack on another girl, I would be furious. I scooted farther away from Jackson on the bed as he continued to argue with Rebecca over the phone about hanging out.

"I'll see you at seven," he finally said.

I watched as he ended the call and placed his cellphone back in his front pocket. Jackson glanced over at me before clearing his throat.

"Anyway, the Imperium Council members are a ruthless bunch," he said.

"You don't say," I laughed. I tossed aside the intimate moment between us and tried to focus on the issue at hand.

"Juliet hates dhampirs. She thinks we're a wasted species. She also hates anyone who tries to invade on her territory. Calix will follow Juliet because he's in love with her. Sebastian will definitely be on your side because he hates Juliet and what she stands for. Noella will be behind you, and Honor is a mystery, because usually she makes her decision last second. Finn is just an arrogant asshole. So, don't expect much from his side. It's Artimis who's going to have the final say, so you need to win him over," he informed.

"What about Theodore and Aurora?" I asked.

"Because he is your mentor and she is his companion they are ruled out of the voting. It would be biased," Jackson explained.

"That's a load of shit," I scoffed.

"I know, but I have no doubt this will work in your favor."

So much confidence, I thought. *He's stupid too.* If I didn't get out of my head, I was going to lose it. Jackson got up from my bed and held out his hand to me.

"Come on, I want to show you something," he said.

I hesitated, a little afraid of what he wanted to "show me."

"Ivy, don't you trust me?"

No, but I couldn't answer and got up anyway, ignoring his hand, and followed him out into the hallway and down the stairs. He opened the front door, and I noticed the blood was gone and so was the body. Not a single trace of that girl was left behind. Part of me felt bad and the other half wanted to drain her dry.

We followed the same path that wrapped around the house into the backyard. I looked up at the sky one last time and mentally kissed the moon goodnight. The grass was wet from the dewiness, and my shoes squeaked with every step. Instead of stopping where we had trained for my meditation session, Jackson veered right near the edge of the woods. He halted just before the path, peeked around at me and smiled.

"What?' I asked.

"I thought I would take you to my favorite place. To help clear your head before they kick you out," he joked.

I stuck out my tongue like a five-year-old, "Ha, you're funny."

He laughed before continuing down the path. The trees made a canopy over us as we walked side by side together. Every once in a while, our fingers would brush up against each other, causing sparks to tingle throughout my body. I wasn't going to deny it, I felt something for him, but what was I to him? Was I a side piece? A mere fling because Rebecca probably treated him shitty? Part of me wanted to ask, though I was afraid to hear the truth, but if I didn't, I was going to drive myself mad. The other part was hoping to avoid the conversation all together and just enjoy the serenity moments with each other. But I knew it wouldn't last forever, even this blissful walk underneath the breezy oak trees.

Jackson continued to guide me along the path. Bats flapped aggressively overhead, and the smell of sap filled the air. Soon, the tree line opened up to a clear, blue river that coursed through a small mountain of rocks. All the oaks glistened in the radiant moonlight. Flowers upon flowers hugged the side of the river. Blues, pinks, yellows, even reds playfully swayed together. A bench faced the view, placed in the middle of the small open field, giving it an idyllic atmosphere. Jackson nudged my shoulder, wanting me to follow him over to the bench. We both sat down and listened to every sound that we could. The small river trickled down through the rocks, glistening like diamonds. The air was calm, and the smells were unforgettable. I was afraid to leave this place. To go back into crazy town and deal with all the bullshit from the Imperium Council. Jackson leaned back against the bench, placing one arm on the back. He looked over at me with such an intense stare, I had to look away.

"So, uh, how did you find this place?" I asked as I tried to avoid his beautiful face.

"I made it," he said proudly.

My mouth dropped forty feet, "You made this place? How?"

"Well, let's see. Home depot had some really great deals on soil and this bench we're sitting on," he joked. I laughed as I patted the smooth wood, mesmerized by the patterns and swirls of it.

"Oh, and here, you're going to need this," said Jackson. He reached in his front pocket and pulled out a vial of blood. Delicious blood. Suddenly, I was very hungry. Licking my lips, I reached over and snagged the vial before Jackson offered it to me. The texture of the liquid was so smooth, I barely felt it go down. Every time I consumed my meal, it filled me with complete ecstasy. I moaned in approval with each flick of my tongue that grazed along my lips, trying to find any small drop that escaped.

"We're going to need to control that," he sighed.

I shifted my eyes to see a disapproving Jackson. "I haven't killed anybody yet."

"Yet," he repeated.

"What do you put in here anyway?"

"Um blood?"

"Besides that."

Jackson paused, the look on his face displayed he was contemplating on telling me the truth. The way his body shifted uncomfortably indicated he was surprised I could tell something was different about the vials of blood. By the looks of it, I don't think he was expecting me to figure it out. Finally, after a long stare down, he took a deep breath and crossed his arms over his chest, "There is something else in the... formula that helps keep your hunger under control. Most dhampirs don't need a higher dose of what we put in, but you, however, show a stronger desire for blood. The idea is, we feed you three times a day of that amount so you can build a tolerance and then eventually have it in moderation."

So, I'm a raging alcoholic... but to blood. Great. "Would I be allowed to feed on... humans?"

Jackson shook his head, "Dhampirs cannot compel, remember? To hunt your prey, you must make sure they forget what happens. You have to be stealthy. Nobody knows we exist. It becomes too much of a liability for the council to control everyone. Someone will slip up."

Well, this is great. He is actually giving me information I so desperately wanted, and yet I couldn't help but feel like I was being babysat. Being a dhampir is one thing, but having limitations on what I could and could not do really put a damper on the whole live forever you can do what you want thingy. I knew Theodore had saved my life, I don't know why, but shouldn't that amount to some kind of freedom? I was being caged like an animal... ironic.

"Jackson... why me?" I whispered. I began to pick at my pants, nervously waiting for him to reply.

Our eyes locked as he bit his lip in concentration, "I don't know, but what I do know is that you're here for a reason. So, don't doubt your existence, okay?"

I nodded and leaned back against the bench. Jackson and I continued to observe the river flow through the rocks. The air around us shifted, creating a cool breeze between the trees. The river echoed softly in the small space between us, which was oddly comforting. Jackson may have been one hundred percent sure of my chance of making it through this verdict, but a part of me couldn't shake the uneasiness as time ticked on. Why did it have to be me? Why couldn't it have been Rebecca? Or some other dhampir who could have stumbled upon that dead girl. Would I be better off losing all of what I know now? Would it save me in the long run? If I did lose my memories would it be all of it? Was that why Jackson acted the way he did? What did he want me to remember?

"Artimis...how old is he?' I asked.

"Artimis used to be a knight. So you do the math," he answered.

My eyes bulged out of their sockets. "A knight?"

"Yeah, but you can't tell. Over the centuries, he had to adapt to keep up with the times. It was in battle he was taken and turned."

"The others?"

"I don't know much, but Juliet was turned in the 17th century. She was a midwife."

I sat in awe, mostly because Juliet used to be human and might not have been a total bitch like she was now. Artimis was a knight. A knight who protected his kingdom but lost the battle of his life to keep the people he cared for safe. There was history in this place. All around, inside and out, and I would be damned to have my memories wiped before I could find out more.

Jackson leaned forward, resting his hands on his knees, "We should get going."

"That time already?"

He nodded, a look of sadness in his eyes. "Unfortunately."

I mentally said goodbye to this little sanctuary, heartbroken that I could forget this place, afraid to ask Jackson if he could show me it again. The walk back through the woods was dreadful and magical at the same time. Dreadful because of the meeting I would soon face, magical because I'd just noticed lanterns hung in the branches, creating a luminous glow down the path. The night air was calm again, and Jackson once again brushed his fingers ever so slightly on mine. Either he did this on purpose, I was just hypersensitive, or I was just grossly observant. He made my heart ache for his touch, and I couldn't understand why. I loved how he walked with confidence whenever he entered a room. The way he tousled his hair when he was asked a direct question. The way his lips would twitch when something funny happened. It was not fair, and my anger got the best of me because the next words out of my mouth were ridiculous.

"So, how long have you and Rebecca been together?" I blurted out.

Jackson skidded to a stop. "Why?"

I stopped with him. "Just curious," I lied. I was fishing for information because I was an idiot.

"Hmm... since she became a dhampir, so fifty years," he said as he started to walk forward again.

I gulped. "Fifty?" *Well, there goes my chance*, I thought. *Like I even had one to begin with.*

"Yeah, I mean she wasn't all bad, you know. Like how I first met you, she had the same spunky attitude," he said.

"That sounds like a shitty compliment," I retorted. I couldn't believe he was comparing me to Rebecca the psycho queen.

"Let's not forget you were a total bitch to me when we met," reminded Jackson.

"Let's ALSO not forget you started it."

Jackson laughed as he playfully hit my shoulder. This was the side of him I wanted all the time but rarely got because he seemed to want to keep up his douchebag persona.

The rest of the way back, we joked about who was more of an ass that night when we reentered the mansion.

My heart stopped when I noticed one of the Imperium Council members stood in the middle of the foyer. If my memory served me well, my guess would be Finn. The scar on his cheek was much more noticeable now in the foyer light. It started from the brow bone, through his right eye down to his jawline. His gray eyes were cold, and he wore an all-black suit that looked like it was tailored to the nines. Finn's dark hair was styled in a short comb over, and just by the look on his face, he seemed to be enjoying this whole charade. Jackson stood between Finn and I, making it known that he wasn't fucking around.

"Finn," said Jackson. I was right.

"Jackson," he replied coolly. Finn pulled out a Zippo lighter and began to flick it in an obnoxious manner.

"A little early, aren't we?" Jackson grumbled.

Finn continued to flick the lighter around, "And your point?"

"So, I would like a few more minutes with Ivy, if you don't mind."

Finn pulled out a cigarette from his breast pocket and lit it. He put the butt to his lips and inhaled the toxins. "Go ahead," Finn said as he exhaled a big puff of smoke into the air.

"Alone," snapped Jackson.

"No can do, pretty boy," stated Finn with another drag from his cigarette.

I watched Jackson's jawline flex in anger. Finn leaned casually against the banister to let us know he wasn't going anywhere.

Without another word between them, Jackson turned around and placed his hands on my shoulders. "Just remember what I said, and you'll be fine." His eyes held mine, and I could feel his anguish. I nodded and touched his hand. I wasn't going to delay this any longer, so I went straight over to Finn and gave him my best fake smile.

"I'm ready," I said enthusiastically.

"Excellent," said Finn as he dropped the butt of the cigarette to the floor and stomped on it.

"Are you serious?"

"We have a maid. Let's go." Finn twirled around like a male ballerina and stalked off toward the other direction. Dick.

I looked back at Jackson one more time and followed the jackass to the many hallways of the mansion until we finally ended up at the threshold of the room with the long table. Finn halted so fast, I smacked right into his stone-like back. I stumbled backward, trying to regain my balance.

Finn glanced back at me before opening the gates of hell. "I collected the delinquent."

"Ivy, please sit," called Artimis from the head of the table. Finn took his seat next to Artimis this time.

All of the Imperium Council were dressed in black, from dresses to well-made suits. They were dressed for my funeral. How sweet. Theodore and Aurora sat on the opposite end of Artimis, both looked at me with indifferent expressions. If this was them playing cool, it absolutely sucked ass. The seat across from Juliet was wide open, which meant that would be my throne to hell. I sulked all the way there. Juliet watched me sit with a smirk on her face. She was a two point oh version of Rebecca. Fantastic.

"Now, before we begin. Ivy, you have a chance to rebuttal on this matter," announced Artimis.

Was he serious? I thought. "Rebuttal? Because it was my fault the dead girl was placed there?" My blood began to boil.

"It wasn't your fault, Ivy," said Noella. Her sweet smile gave me some kind of unspoken comfort.

"Can we get to the voting please?" commented Juliet. She tapped her nails vigorously on the wooden table.

"Now, Juliet, Ivy deserves a rebuttal," reminded Artimis.

She rolled her eyes and leaned back into her chair, giving me the stank eye.

Artimis turned to me and motioned for me to speak.

"Who am I going to tell? I don't even know what's going on! If anything, I just want to continue on like nothing ever happened." There, that should convince them.

"How do we know we can trust you?" questioned Calix. Juliet smiled at him sweetly and rubbed his arm. Ah yes, the Calix and Juliet romance. Gross.

"Ivy?" prompted Artimis.

"You CAN trust me, because I don't want anything to do with your secrets," big fat lie, "so, if you don't mind, I would like the vote to happen now so I can go back to my room."

"You heard the girl, Artimis," laughed Finn.

Artimis eyed me from the seat, studying my face. "As you wish."

He rose from his chair, his long black robe covering his tall physique in an attractive way. The top of his hair was slicked back with some type of gel, and you could tell he enjoyed the attention of everyone in the room.

"Those who vote yes to have Ivy's memories erased, say I," he instructed.

"I," hissed Juliet.

"I," agreed Calix.

"I," sneered Finn.

"Those who vote no to have Ivy's memory erased, say I."

"I" said Noella.

"I," whispered Honor.

"I," murmured Sebastian.

I took a good look around the table. The I's were divided equally, and it gave me a clear view on who was by my side and who wasn't.

"I guess that leaves me," said Artimis matter-of-factly.

My whole body was on edge, waiting for the final verdict. I prayed Jackson was right, and this would be in my favor.

"Ivy, I believe people deserve second chances, but be advised. If we catch you near something like this again, we won't hesitate to remove what has been seen," he warned.

A wave of relief washed over me when Artimis said those words.

"You have got to be fucking kidding me!" Juliet barked. She rose from the table, ready to strike.

"Juliet," soothed Calix. Juliet brushed off his hand and crossed right over to me, leaning into my face.

"Listen here, sweetheart, if I catch you snooping ONCE in this place, you're done!" Juliet stomped dramatically out of the room with Calix on her trail.

"Ignore Juliet, she likes to make a scene, always," said Noella. I stood and faced her. She was even more gorgeous up close. Her turquoise eyes sparkled in the hazy light, and her hair was a vibrant violet color that fell in perfect waves down her back.

I gazed around and noticed everyone had left the room, including Theodore and Aurora. "Where did everyone go?"

"To work," she said nonchalantly.

"Oh."

"I'm sorry Theodore is avoiding you. He's having a hard time adjusting without his former dhampir."

"So it would seem."

Noella patted my shoulder and smiled down at me, "Hey, listen, if you ever need someone to talk to, don't hesitate. My room is in this wing on the second floor. Third door away from the women's bathroom."

"Thanks."

"You're one lucky dhampir. No has ever been saved from compulsion." She waved me goodbye and left the room. I stood alone, looking around at the paintings I hadn't seen before. All the faces on the walls were of the council, even Jackson was on there. I ran my hand over the detailed frames and continued down the line, reading the little blurbs on the plaques. One face that I hadn't seen before made me do a double take. He had really short red hair and dark eyes. His freckles were of millions on his face, and for some reason, he looked oddly familiar to me. I read his plaque, but the only thing on there was a name.

"Rowan," I whispered. Not even a memory was triggered when I said it out loud. *How do I know you?* I thought.

Artimis' warning crept up on me like a lion to its prey. I decided tonight was not the night for more investigation, and I left the room. The first person I wanted to tell was Jackson. He was right after all, and it would only be fair to tell him the good news first. I kind of half-assed walked through the two hallways leading back out to the foyer. The excitement was exploding from within as I ran up the stairs to the dhampir side of the house. *Is he in one of these rooms?* I thought. Truth was, I'd never seen him in one before. He would always come and get me. One of the doors down the hall to the left was cracked open. Some soft moans were coming from inside. I tiptoed slowly, trying not to intrude, but couldn't help but be curious. The sounds grew louder as I got closer, shadows moved in weird patterns on the wall. I peeked into the slightly ajar door and instantly regretted it.

Two bodies rolled around on the bed until one of them straddled the other. Her platinum blonde hair was a dead giveaway, and I suddenly recognized the two individuals in the act. Jackson held Rebecca by the waist as he pounded right into her. She leaned forward into him, kissing his neck and chest. Moans escaped from both of them as the air filled with the smell of sex. Anger and jealousy made my chest and throat tight, and from what I could see, he was still very much *into* Rebecca. Sick to my stomach, I turned right around and made it to my bedroom without keeling over. I collapsed onto my bed and began an ugly cry. Overwhelmed by everything else around me, watching Jackson that way with Rebecca was the icing on the cake. I knew I wasn't stupid, there was something else Jackson wasn't telling me. The feelings I would get around him, the way he looked at me. Personally, I should just move on and stop wishing he would come to my team. Why did I feel so strongly for this guy? Had I been like this as a human? Was this a strong trait that passed over? Feeling completely and utterly disgusted with myself, I twisted the lamp off, got under the covers, and decided the only way to overcome this bullshit was to sleep. Again.

CHAPTER 12

The rest of the weekend went by in a massive blur. I remember waking up from my extra nap and seeing a name badge hanging from my doorknob with another note from Theodore, along with a uniform—a black polo, khakis, and the note stating work began at one and would end at five. Apparently, Jackson would be my chauffeur to and from work, since Theodore kept dodging me. I tried his office several times throughout the day, yet he was never there.

Gypsy stopped by a few times and mentioned that as a "dhampir" we got special human meals and we could request anything we wanted. She also mentioned we would be gathering in the great room, unknown to me at that time—it was the room I'd had my verdict in. Talk about PTSD. Gypsy said it wasn't often we were allowed to have human food, they wanted us to build our strength and tolerance to blood. It seemed they wanted us to be more vampire than human, but I guess some of the dhampirs didn't like that and rebelled against a strict hemoglobin diet. I received more information from Gypsy than my own mentor, so it really went to show how much he actually cared. I hid in my room most of the time, only opening it for Zach, since he became delivery boy for my vial of blood. I guess Jackson had some work to do and couldn't stop by. I called that a lame ass excuse, since I was convinced he knew I was the one who'd walked in on him and Rebecca doing the nasty. Zach would sit with me and talk about his early years of being a dhampir, which gave me a better view on what I truly was.

"Before they gave us the stupid vial system, we could feed on humans, and the vampires would compel them. We did everything in moderation too," he said.

"Really? Why did they change?" I asked.

"Because Artimis showed up, that's why," Zach sighed.

The way Zach said Artimis' name, indicated more than just pure annoyance. Zach would not continue with the conversation, and I didn't want to press it any further. We said our goodbyes for the afternoon until my next feeding.

As I prepared for work, I contemplated on skipping out to hide in my room. Was I avoiding work? No, I was trying to avoid Jackson as much as possible. Maybe he wouldn't mention it at all. Maybe he'd been so preoccupied with *who* he was doing, he hadn't suspected my presence. I reached for my uniform and tried to put it on as slowly as I could, fixing each button with delicate hands. Ridiculous as it might be, I could not face him, not yet.

The afternoon light shimmied its way in through the thick curtains, making little silhouettes of the trees' branches on my wall. As fall busted its way in, so did the cold weather. Since I was only a dhampir, according to Gypsy, the cold still bothered us, not as much as an actual human, but just enough to need a light jacket. Vampires had no problem in the cold, but from what I could understand with my last encounter with them, they loved their robes.

I hadn't seen any vampires since my "trial," and that made me feel relieved, but I was warned to stay out of what was going on. Thankfully, Gypsy had gone undercover and was going to steal the books from the library. I brushed back my hair and decided to put it in a ponytail, pinching my cheeks for some color. I rummaged through my dresser and found a powder-blue lightweight jacket. I stuffed my arms through the sleeves and zipped it halfway up. It was interesting how they had all my sizes perfectly set up. With a little mascara and lip balm, I was good to go. Clipping the name tag on my collar, I stole one more glance at the clock; it read four-fifteen. I shook off the anxiety, swallowed my pride, and made my way downstairs to the foyer. Jackson leaned casually against the threshold of the front door, typing away furiously on his phone.

"I'm ready," I announced.

"Good, let's go." Not one look from Jackson, he rushed down the front steps to his black truck.

Okay then, I thought. I hopped into the passenger seat as he put the truck into drive, speeding through the back roads like a mad man. I glanced over at him, watching his sour face focus on the path in front of us. He wore a gray sweatshirt and faded blue jeans. His hair was tousled in a way that made him look like he'd just rolled out of bed. A five o'clock shadow had begun to shade his jawline. He was quiet for a while but made small grunting noises when someone would cut in front of him. Jackson would aggressively fix his hair whenever he held back from swearing.

"You good?" I asked.

"Yeah, fine. Here," he said as he reached into his pocket, one hand on the steering wheel, "Theodore got you a cellphone so we can keep in touch while you're at work. Only contacts are myself, him, Aurora, and the manager whose name is Earl." He handed me a black phone. I pressed the home button and discovered it was a simple little device with no passcode.

"Thanks" I mumbled.

"So, next time it will be easier to text me, instead of barging in while I'm trying to make love to my girlfriend," explained Jackson.

My heart skidded to a stop against my ribcage. *Fuck,* I thought. Jackson looked over at me, waiting for an explanation. My palms began to sweat, and my mouth had gone dry from the anxiety, while the flame ignited on my cheeks was not from the heat in the car.

"I di... didn't know," I stuttered.

"Next time you will," he snapped.

"What the fuck is your problem?" *That's it,* I thought.

"My only problem is people not respecting my privacy."

"Sorry, I wasn't expecting to find you banging your bitch of a girlfriend."

Jackson pulled over to a curb. My guess was we had arrived at my work, but I was too pissed to even ask. He had more mood swings than an actual girl.

"I'll pick you up at five, and I'll text you when I'm outside," he stated.

"K," was all I said when I hopped out and slammed the passenger door. Jackson revved his truck and drove down the street out of sight.

Without another thought, I decided the smart thing to do was to text the manager I was there rather than trying to figure out where I needed to go and end up lost. Especially since I was angry, and I didn't want to hurt anyone.

The factory consisted of four brick buildings all lined neatly on the strip of some small-town shopping plaza. It didn't really look like a typical factory on the outside, more like brick apartments you would find in a city. The area around the factory was completely vacant. I was the only person standing outside. Of course, I still didn't know my exact location, but the town itself was quiet and had a home-like feeling to it. Something one would see in a Hallmark movie. I reached into my right pocket on my jacket and texted the manager that I was there. My phone buzzed not two seconds after I sent the text letting me know he would be down in a minute. The front door to the middle part of the building creaked open to reveal a man in a striped, button-down shirt and blue overalls that went over it. He had little to no hair on top of his head, and when he smiled, I could see a few missing teeth. I awkwardly smiled back as he approached me.

"The name's Earl," he said as he reached for my hand.

Our hands clasped, and I realized he was warm and pulsating. *Shit*, I thought. *A human.* My throat tingled a little bit from the smell that came off his skin but not enough to make me attack his throat. It looked like the "special formula" Zach had given me earlier was working.

"Ivy," I said.

"Follow me, and I'll show you around," said Earl.

Earl led me inside and began to point out rooms and people.

"This is Elaine. Elaine is our secretary, so whatever you need, she will be at your service," he introduced.

An older woman with grayish-white hair smiled and waved from inside her office through a large glass window. She had on black pants and a matching black blazer with several pins attached to the collar.

"Certain days of the week, Elaine has an assistant who helps her with the filing and phone calls," We continued down the hall, and Earl stopped in front of a cafeteria off to the left.

"And this is where we eat our meals," he stated.

Earl gestured toward the wide setting arrangement before us. About a dozen round tables with plastic blue chairs surrounded it's perimeter. Vending machines and a salad bar were placed neatly in the middle. I noticed a few workers in the area who swept or wiped down the tables.

"Lunch is over so they're preparing for dinner," mentioned Earl.

I nodded as if I knew that was what they were doing. He waved me on down the rest of the hall, pointing out the bathrooms and locker room where the workers left their stuff during their shift. The whole front part of the factory was just a small office type setting, very normal. All the walls were cream colored, and a few weird paintings helped fill up the empty space. We reached the end of the hall at a door that said *staff only* in big bolded letters.

"Here is where the magic begins," he said excitedly. Earl turned the knob and began to descend down a flight of stairs. Trailing right behind him, we came to a set of double steel doors with a sign that said *keep out, top secret area*. Earl turned around and grinned like a little boy in a candy shop.

"You ready?" he asked.

"Um... sure," I laughed.

He released the hatch on the doors and shoved them open to reveal a two-story factory room with shelves filled to the brim with boxes. We entered from the top floor and walked over to the railing to stare down at the line of workers cranking machines and filling boxes. Some gave orders, others were rotating the bottles, checking for cracks or misprints. All the workers had on white lab coats and hairnets. There were four long processing stations, all set up the same. Each section of station there were at least five people doing the same job. The aroma of the human fragrance hung in the air, but not enough to make me hungry. I made a mental note to ask Jackson what exactly was in the formula, if we ever spoke again.

Earl tapped my shoulder to have me follow him down the stairs and led me toward the beginning of the first workstation where a few of the workers were stirring some type of liquid inside.

"We stir the mixture here," he pointed to two gigantic tanks of red wine, "and we drain them from these tanks to the filter tubes, making sure no seeds from the grapes are stuck," he pointed up to two spiraled, clear tubes connecting all the way down to the tanks. "Next," as we walked down the line, "they go through another filter that connects to one tank where the secret formula is mixed together," he tapped the center tank labeled *black sheep ink*. "After that, they are poured equally into these wine bottles," I watched the burgundy colored wine circle through another set of clear tubes. A smaller machine was lined up perfectly with the top of each bottle as it poured the right amount of wine into each one. "The machine then takes it down the belt to have the corks pressed into the top, and then it gets a nice label smacked on it by our label machine. At the end of this line, we have experts making sure everything is sealed and labeled correctly. Any imperfections, it goes into the damage pile," Earl finished.

My head felt dizzy from all the information. This whole system was orchestrated so precisely, I was afraid to even look at the merchandise. Theodore, the Imperium Council, whoever did this was not fucking around.

"As you can see, there are three more stations. We have two different reds and two different whites," he said.

I nodded and walked over, looking inside the tank with the white wine. The smell was inviting, and I remembered I would be able to taste it. Some of the workers smiled at me politely, others were so engrossed with their work, they had no idea I was around them. The whole system seemed to flow with ease, and I found it quite comical that I, Ivy, a dhampir, would be granted eternal life just to help out at a factory which was ran by the most uptight group of vampires I had ever met.

Earl caught my attention and motioned for me to come back to where he was standing. When I reached him, I noticed a petite blonde with big brown eyes hid under her square shaped glasses. She also wore a white lab coat and a hairnet that wrapped around her perfectly tight bun.

"Ivy, I want you to meet Patricia Stonewall. She is in charge of all the workstations in this facility," introduced Earl.

Patricia reached for my hand and gave it a firm shake, "Ivy, it is so nice to meet you. Theodore said you have great drive and would be a fantastic asset to our team."

"Oh, well yeah, that's me," I said awkwardly. *Of course he would talk me up*, I thought.

"Well, it was nice meetin' you. I gotta get back to work," said Earl. With a quick wave to the both of us, he departed back up the steps.

"Earl is manager to our loading dock," stated Patricia. For a man with such poor taste in his fashion, it actually made sense.

"Would you like to see your office?" she asked.

"My office?"

"I'm guessing Theodore forgot to mention you get an office. It's small, but it's for you to use when going over paperwork. You'll also be charged with hiring new people." Patricia said.

I shrugged my shoulders. "I guess so."

"Let me show you your office and some of the work you'll be doing, and after that, we can have you try a new wine." Patricia motioned for me to follow her through another door that said *staff only*. The hallway lit up white walls and tiles and multiple offices with peoples' names engraved on the doors. A few employees passed by us and greeted Patricia and myself. We made it to the end of the hall in front of a brown door with no name on the glass. Patricia looked over and smiled at me before unlocking it with a key kept in her front pocket.

"It's a little bit dusty, but we asked the cleaning service to come tomorrow in the morning to freshen it up." Patricia stepped aside for me to enter first.

The room was a simple four corner office with one small basement window. Cream-colored walls and a brown desk with a black swivel chair completed the room. The walls were bare and the floors were hardwood. Everything was so ordinary it reminded me of the bedroom I'd stayed in at the cottage. Suddenly wished I was there right now.

"I left some papers on your desk. Just a few things to sign off on." She walked over to pull out the swivel chair, "Come, sit."

I walked over and sat down in the surprisingly soft swivel chair, pushed myself in, and looked down at the small stack of papers in the middle of the desk.

"This is just standard procedure. Just some liability forms, and you'll be good to go. I indicated where to sign," Patricia reached forward and flipped through the pages, landing on one with a line that said *sign here*. An x was marked off next to the line. She leaned in and handed me a pen. Her neck was suddenly in my line of sight and I could see her vein pulsating against her soft skin. My mouth began to water, and my hands shook when I took the pen from her, "After you sign that, there are two more in the next couple of pages, and you'll be all set."

I tore my eyes from her neck long enough to gain composure and realized as I was about to sign, I had no idea what my last name was. Between the sudden hunger and awkward silence, I just wanted to get the fuck out of there.

"Is there a problem?" she asked.

I gulped. "Nope." The hunger tickled my throat.

With shaking hands, I signed my first name. I tried to make my first name as long as possible, trailing off at the end so it showed I had a last name when I really didn't. I skimmed through the rest and signed them all the exactly same way and handed her back the pen and packet. Clearly, she had no idea I was a dhampir, otherwise I wouldn't be signing this useless crap.

"Excellent! Now, let's go over your daily routine. It is quite simple. You do interviews in the morning. Don't worry, we have a list of questions you ask the interviewee, and if they meet those requirements, then we make the decision of hiring them. Next, you head over to the workstations, and you make sure all the employees are wearing their uniforms and gear correctly. You monitor them as well at each station. We want all our employees to be on the same page, so if someone is not doing their job right, we want to know asap. Once the cart is filled with the wine bottles, it is your job to do one final check and taste test. This means the labels are on correctly, the corks are secured, and the wine doesn't have grape seeds. If one bottle has seeds, the rest are most likely to be victims," said Patricia.

My mind spun as she relayed the information to me. Here I was, struggling not to rip her neck apart, and I was being told I would have to become a working member of society. This whole situation was ass-backward, but I couldn't do anything about it. *Yet*, I thought. *There's no way our kind has always been like this.*

I gazed up at Patricia and smiled. "That sounds easy."

"I trust you will help us greatly." She touched my shoulder and gave it a light squeeze. The veins on her arm flexed, and I swallowed hard, fighting the urge to drain every ounce out of her. Just as I grew paranoid that the formula might not be working anymore, Patricia released her grip on me and walked over to the door, "Let's begin."

I wiped the sweat from my forehead and followed her out. I inhaled and exhaled deep breaths as we made our way back to the four stations. The phone in my pocket buzzed, but I was too focused on my breathing to break the trance and check if there was a message. Once we got back out on the front line, the air became easier to breathe. I took a deep breath to get rid of the last trace of anxiety from my body. Not so hyper focused on Patricia's neck anymore, we headed over to the last station. She greeted a tall man with the same white coat as hers. They exchanged a quick conversation before he disappeared.

"Kevin, our supervisor, is going to get us some cups for you to taste the product," she said.

Maybe this will take the edge off, I thought.

Kevin came back and handed us each a clear plastic cup. Patricia was then handed the bottle of wine, and she pulled the cork with a pocket wine key.

"May I?" Patricia held out her hand for my cup. I gave it to her and watched her twist the bottle to expose the label. The label was black with gold embroidery and a golden rose printed in the center. As she began to pour, my mind became fuzzy. My vision was spotty, and a sharp pain shot across my temple. I went blind as my eyesight adjusted with the new picture in front of me.

I was standing in the middle of a beautifully decorated living room. This time, I was myself in the memory. Silver garlands hung from the door frames and a banister. A man sat in a recliner, sipped gingerly from a Santa Claus mug. His reddish-brown hair was slicked back, and he had the tip of a pipe in his mouth. Slight wrinkles hugged the corners of his bright eyes. I giggled as I watched a cute older boy dig through a box of assorted decorations. The boy smiled at me when he placed an ornament perfectly on one of the lower branches. He had on a checkered sweater vest, and the smell of sugar cookies hung in the air. I wore a beautiful red dress and a white cardigan. Everything *felt* perfect. Excitement radiated through me and the little boy. He had a wide eye gaze whenever he picked up an ornament and examined the details. I would watch him and help direct him toward the right spot on the tree. A woman appeared with a bottle of wine and two glasses. She wore a black glitter dress that complimented her curves and her dark, brown hair waved at her back. She was beautiful, and I stared at her in awe. She handed the gentlemen in his chair a glass and began to pour the dazzling red liquid to the brim. Suddenly, the memory began to fade, spinning me back toward reality. As if my mind couldn't keep up with my movements, Patricia handed me the red plastic cup, and it slipped from my hand. The contents splashed the floor in crimson red, staining not only myself, but Patricia and Kevin as well. I stood there, unaware of my actions, until I heard the "oh dears" break my conscious.

I looked down and saw a few employees scramble to clean up my mess. The wine splattered in different directions, creating a wine stain mess everywhere. Patricia came over to me and touched my face. Her warm hand against my clammy face made me flinch. "Are you okay, dear?" Her voice echoed inside my head as I tried to piece together what had just happened. A slight ringing sound vibrated inside my right eardrum when I moved my head. My eyes stung from the lights inside the factory, and sweat trickled on my eyebrows.

"Yeah," I managed to say. *Am I?* I thought.

"Maybe you should go home early today. Get some rest. You look a little pale," stated Patricia.

Automatically, my hand patted my cheek, embarrassed because I'd made a huge scene.

"Are you sure?" I said weakly.

"Yes, and if you're still not feeling well by tomorrow, just text Earl. Okay?"

"Okay." I must have really looked rough if she was trying to send me home.

I reached in my jacket pocket and found a text message from Jackson.

Jackson: How's the first day?

Too mentally drained to argue about his niceness toward me again, I replied back:

Me: Fine. I was let go a little early today. Can you pick me up?

Not a few seconds later, my phone vibrated.

Jackson: Yes.

Weak and pretty parched, I said my goodbyes to Patricia and the crew and made my way upstairs. I had to grip the railing for support, afraid I would topple backward and cause an even bigger scene. How embarrassing was this? First day on the job, and I ended up in flashback mode. That little boy with the loose curls and the cheesy grin. The woman in my memory was so strikingly beautiful, it made my chest ache. The wine bottle she held was the exact same one at this factory. What are the odds both those moments would collide? And who was that guy in the recliner? Was he with the lady in black? I reached the top and pushed through the double doors and walked the rest of the way in small strides. Somehow, my old life was connected to my new one. I didn't know how or why, but there had to be a reason. I knew once Gypsy retrieved those books, it would all start to make sense. Right now, the best thing I could do was act as normal as possible and try to get the flashbacks under control.

I waved goodbye to Elaine before stepping out into the late afternoon air. Thankfully, I refrained from annihilating poor Patricia. If I'd chosen to execute her then and there, it would have probably been all over for Theodore and the council. The "formula" that was mixed with the blood I took clearly was not measuring up to its job. How much would I need to actually be able to stay around humans and not try to murder them? Would the Imperium Council lock me up? Would they end me for trying to end others? This all had become too complicated in a matter of days.

Jackson's black truck pulled up just in time, before I decided to have a mental breakdown. I climbed in and found a somber looking Jackson.

"You okay?" he asked. I could tell he was studying my face.

"Fine," I lied. I was not about to go into details with the mood swings king himself.

"Here, I brought you dinner." Jackson held out a vial of blood for me to take.

"Thanks." Before another word could pass between us, I downed all of it in one gulp. The blood filled my veins, electrifying my senses and calming my mind all at the same time. If my human self-saw this, I bet twenty bucks she would puke.

"Better?" he asked. As if Jackson knew that was what I'd truly needed.

"Yeah," I wiped my mouth, "just letting you know, I don't think the formula is working anymore."

Jackson watched me intensely. "How so?"

"I almost ate my boss for lunch," I joked.

Jackson's eyes sparkled. "I wish I'd been there to see that."

His comment caught me off guard. *Bipolar much?* I thought. I wasn't going to jinx his good mood, so I just chuckled as he put the truck in drive, and we headed out of town.

CHAPTER 13

I became restless for the next couple of days. Strictly based on the fact that I couldn't get that memory out of my head. It would appear at the most inconvenient times, too. At work was the worst. I ended up going back the next day, feeling better, but nervous. I conducted a few interviews in the morning for a couple of shifts. One was more awkward than the next, but I managed to make it through. Each person who came in all had the same mindset; I'm desperate for money. I felt bad and maybe a little envious. To only worry about not having enough money would have been a better trade off then having the constant fear of ripping someone's neck apart.

The worst part about that was being in close proximity to the interviewees, because the aroma coming off their skin would penetrate my concentration, and I was trying not to murder everyone who walked through the door. All the interviews so far had lasted about an hour; I managed but just barely. Around the three-thirty mark was the part I dreaded the most. It was the wine testing time, and I would have to nonchalantly avoid Kevin, our assistant manager, pouring us the cup of the product. Anything to prevent a triggered memory and embarrassing myself again was the goal for every shift. Eventually, I got to try it, and I could taste the slight undertone of the blood in the wine. It definitely wasn't human blood, human blood had a sweet taste almost like liquid sugar, but vampire blood was tangier. I could now understand why the product sold so well.

After every shift, Jackson would be precisely on time to pick me up at five, almost like clockwork. Our car rides weren't so bad, but few words were exchanged about what I did at my job. Theodore was still gone. Whenever I would ask around about his whereabouts, I would get the same response; he would be out of his office or on another business trip. For now, Jackson was both my mentor and trainer; a double pain in my ass.

Today, after work, Jackson picked me up and brought me back to the mansion grounds for another meditation session. I was getting really sick of them, but Jackson said it would be good for my mind to have better focus and control over my hunger so they could lessen the formula.

We sat crossed legged him and I, our eyes both closed as we breathed in the autumn air. The trees had begun to deepen in color; reds, yellows, and oranges. Everything was vibrant compared to us and our pale complexions. Our sessions would always start the same; I would clear my mind of any negativity and then we would proceed to worst case scenarios and how to solve them. I honestly thought this was all bullshit because no matter how much I tried, the hunger would always be there; taunting me. The desire still lingered in my mind. My body reacted to it almost automatically when the scent would hit the brim of my nose. If I wasn't heavily supervised, we would be looking at a body count in the hundreds at this point.

Jackson tapped my forehead to get my attention. "I want to try something new."

The look he gave me already told me it wasn't going to be a good idea. "And that is?"

Jackson waved a vial of blood in front of my face. "This batch doesn't have the formula. This is pure human blood."

I gulped. Pure human blood. If I wasn't an addict by now, I was going to be sent to rehab after this.

"Ivy, we need to control your hunger," he said.

I picked at the grass. "I know."

"Close your eyes again. And remember what I've been teaching you. Clear the mind of negativity. Inhale and exhale deeply. Center yourself," instructed Jackson.

As if I'd done this a hundred times before, I followed Jackson's instructions without complaint. My body felt less tense after I did the breathing warm-ups, but I wasn't about to admit that to him.

"I'm going to uncork the vial," he said.

The pop sound was all I needed to make my anxiety appear. *I can do this*, I thought. For the safety of others, and to make sure the Imperium Council doesn't have an easy excuse to execute me, I had to get this under control.

"I'm going to move closer, so the smell can reach you," said Jackson.

My fists were clenched so tightly from anticipation, I could have sworn I popped a few veins in my knuckles.

Right on cue, the smell hitched up in my throat and made it burn with an undeniable thirst. It was stronger this time, more potent than the mixed supply. I tried to imagine myself in a calm place like a beach or the sanctuary Jackson showed me a few nights back. But no matter how hard I focused, it would invade my conscious, pulling me under like a tidal wave. What started out as a small flame, turned into a structure fire; unstoppable and deadly. When my eyes opened, they focused on one thing and one thing only; that vial. Before I could stop myself, I lunged forward at Jackson, stealing it from his grasp.

"Shit!" he exclaimed.

We tossed around on the blanket, before I kicked him in the stomach to paralyze him long enough to drink it.

The vial was empty, and the fire was out. The blood coursed through me, filling me up with a sensation so powerful, a frenzy began. I felt high and completely at bliss. The human blood was much more intense than I'd thought. It gave me purpose—it gave me life. The blood was the only thing that made me feel alive. But it always made me dangerous and put me two steps back from where I was before. Coming down from the high, I was ashamed of my actions. Ashamed that I let down Jackson. I glanced sideways at him, afraid to speak.

"Well, I knew it wasn't going to be easy, but I didn't realize how short your will power would be."

"I'm sorry," I mumbled.

"Maybe next time, I'll handcuff you." Our eyes locked and I could sense he meant more behind the comment then he entailed. It gave me weird stomach flips; a feeling I couldn't deny.

"Ivy."

"Yeah?"

"What's really bothering you? You seem distant."

Have I? Was it that obvious? I continued to pick at the grass. "I'm good."

A deep sigh rattled in Jackson's chest. "I know I'm not the most pleasant person to be around, but you can talk to me, you know?"

All I could do was stare at his pretty blue eyes. There was no way in hell I could mention the memories and the sweet desire to rip his clothes off. I made a promise to myself that the only person I could trust in this place was Gypsy. Until Jackson gave me a reason to, it was a no go. As for the feelings, well, they would forever be buried inside a locked chest, ten feet underground. I didn't need another reason for Rebecca wanting me dead. Sometimes it was hard, he would do certain things or talk to me in a way that had me constantly second guessing myself.

Jackson uncrossed his legs and rose to his feet, gathering the materials we'd used today for our session.

"I'm sorry," I said again.

"For what?" He looked down at me with a confused expression. A very cute, confused expression.

"Just, everything," I shrugged.

He scratched his head and looked around as if he was having a hard time trying to respond. To spare him the trouble, I decided to join him in picking up the materials, and we both silently walked back to the mansion. Jackson was a man of many things but expressing his feelings was not one of them.

Laughter echoed through the foyer from the dhampir rec room, making me jump. Jackson collected the rest of the stuff from me and disappeared without another word. There was a good chance I'd hurt his feelings, but there was a better chance of trust being broken.

I followed the sound of laughter to see Zach, Gypsy, Tyler, and Justin laughing around the seating area. Gypsy noticed me first and patted the seat next to her on the couch.

"Hey, girlie!" she said excitedly. Gypsy slung her arm over my shoulder and gave it a right squeeze.

"All good," I lied. Definitely not the best time or place to discuss hidden desires and secrets with Gypsy.

"Aye, Ivy, has Jackson bruised you yet?" cackled Justin.

"Nah, dude, Ivy definitely kicks his ass," teased Tyler.

I rolled my eyes. "What's the catch?"

They both looked at each other and erupted into laughter. "It's not what we heard,"

"It's what we SAW." Both keeled over until Zach kicked them both in the shins.

"I can't believe the marketing company for the business is run by you two clowns," scoffed Zach.

I turned to Gypsy with a confused look.

"Tyler and Justin are really good at selling the product. So, they're in charge of going door to door and training others to do the same," she explained.

"Isn't it a bit strange how we're immortal, but have *normal* jobs?" I questioned.

Gypsy shrugged. "I guess."

Zach looked over at me and placed his finger to his lips, indicating for me to be quiet. I looked over at him, puzzled, but he averted his eyes from me. *What the fuck was that?* I thought.

The door to the rec room swung open to Rebecca strutting dramatically across the room while dragging Jackson along by his hand. It ripped a hole in my heart as both sat opposite us on the couch with Rebecca half straddling Jackson's body. It was a struggle having to constantly remind myself that it could never happen, and I needed to accept that. She looked over at me and smirked before nibbling on his ear. Jackson leaned away from her and made eye contact with me. I squirmed under his gaze, waiting for someone to break the silence.

"So, Ivy," sneered Rebecca, trying to gain my attention away from Jackson.

Here we go. "Yeah?"

"I hear you have a blood addiction."

Are you fucking kidding me? I glared at Jackson, pissed he had the nerve to talk behind my back. His eyes bored into mine, making the pit of my stomach jump. *What is wrong with him?*

"What's your point, Rebecca?" interjected Zach.

"I just find it funny, that's all. We got a little junkie in the group. It's only a matter of time now before she kills someone," she said.

"Rebecca, go to hell," snapped Gypsy.

"I love how you all talk for her. Super cute," laughed Rebecca.

The door opened again as three dhampirs entered the room. Three new dhampirs made up the nine. The nine that Gypsy said were living here with besides myself.

Both the guys were strikingly good looking, the first one who walked in had dark, shoulder length hair and bright eyes. His skin was milky white, and his outfit screamed motorcycle gang. He had a lip ring and a snake tattoo on his neck. When his eyes landed on me, he smirked and gave me a little wink. The second male who came in had beautiful chocolate skin and a sky-high Afro. He pounded fists with the twins and Zach before leaning against the pool table. Last was a female with flaming red hair half shaved on one side, she had a nose ring and thick winged eyeliner that made her brown eyes look huge. The chick also rocked the motorcycle style. She walked over to stand behind Rebecca, and it was pretty clear they were besties.

"Mabel, you missed one hell of a conversation," said Rebecca.

"Oh really? Do tell," she demanded. Mabel's eyes scanned over to me, giving me the same smirk of mockery that Rebecca did.

"She's a blood addict," Rebecca cackled.

"Ha! Knew it."

Gypsy gave Rebecca the death stare but only mildly glanced at the girl named Mabel. Their exchange was brief but noticeable enough for me to want to question Gypsy about it later.

I was in no way in a good enough mood to deal with this high school charade and too emotionally drained to handle this shit, I got up and planned on storming out of there, when Finn stepped over the threshold, cat walking to us. He wore dress pants and a half opened pink dress shirt revealing stubble on his chest. Another cigarette in hand, he brisked by me to stand in the middle of the room.

"Listen up boys and girls," he said. Everyone's attention was fixated on him. He twirled around a few times to make sure we were listening.

"Artimis wants extra patrols for the next couple of weeks. So, you gentlemen need to divide up the posts."

All the men besides Jackson exchanged concerned looks.

"Just a few missing people in the area. We want to make sure no nomads are sneaking by us," assured Finn. I knew the minute the words left his lips he was lying. This all boiled down to the dead girls with the marks. The Imperium Council wanted to hide anything they deem suspicious before the rest found out. But I knew the truth, so did Gypsy and Jackson.

"How many bodies?" asked the biker boy.

"Now, Trent, you know I can't reveal that," said Finn. He wagged his finger at him like a schoolteacher.

"Seriously? That's shit. We should be informed," he complained.

"It's none of your fucking business, Trent," snapped Jackson.

The whole room fell silent. All eyes were going back and forth between them, waiting for one to retaliate.

Trent locked his stare with Jackson and just laughed. "Funny, coming from the councils' little bitch boy."

Jackson pushed Rebecca's leg off him to get in Trent's face. Simultaneously, all the men, excluding Finn, tried to hold back the both of them before someone got punched.

Finn turned toward me and said, "Just a reminder for you, sweet cheeks, the council is watching." He took one long drag before throwing it on the floor and stomping on it. Finn gave one last look to the testosterone filled showdown before leaving his mess behind.

"Men," Mabel scoffed.

"My man looks so hot when he's pissed," swooned Rebecca.

I wanted to kick her in the teeth.

"Alright, enough!" demanded Zach.

Jackson and Trent were dragged protectively across the room from each other. Zach had the middle ground, looking back and forth between the heavy breathing gorillas.

"What the fuck is wrong with you two?"

"Ask king shit of fuck mountain over there," snapped Trent.

Jackson tried to lung forward, but Tyler and Justin had him locked in place. "Honestly, Trent, you're a fucking pussy."

"Sooooo tough. I'm out of here. Let me know what my post is." He shrugged out of the other kids' grips and left, slamming the door.

"Babe," cooed Rebecca. She got up and caressed his cheek and kissed his pouty mouth.

Jackson pushed off the hands that were holding him and stormed out of the room. Rebecca gave Mabel a quick look before following after him.

"Nolan," said Zach.

"Yeah," he said, walking over from where he'd stood with Trent. He was a good-looking guy. Flawless chocolate skin with deep-set brown eyes.

"Keep an eye on Trent. I don't want him murdering Jackson in the middle of the night," he said.

"Will do," laughed Nolan as he made his way out the room.

"I'm going to my room," Zach announced. He left Gypsy and I on the couch with the twins arm wrestling in the corner. Mabel popped a piece of gum in her mouth and sat down on the couch.

"Shouldn't the vampires be doing patrols? Aren't they stronger?" I asked.

"The vampires in this coven are l-a-z-y," Mabel responded. She blew a bubble bigger than my head before popping it.

"Only with a serious threat would they intervene," added Gypsy.

"Or one of us dies."

CHAPTER 14

I woke up to the stillness of the house, not even the floorboards creaked when everything settled.

Last night's drama for assigning patrols had really caused a stir between the male dhampirs and had planted an obnoxious smile on Finn's perfect face. He'd known what he was doing, but that hadn't stopped him from igniting the fire.

Today was a new day, and I wasn't going to let it go to waste from something I had no part in.

A slight knock on my door made me jump. The sound of a piece of paper slid under my door across from where I lay. *Strange*, I thought. I tossed the covers aside and reached down to retrieve the paper. It was folded in half with my name written elegantly on the front. I unfolded the letter to find a few sentences in the same script. It read:

Ivy, just got word from the factory that you won't be needed today. Enjoy this day off. I'll speak with you soon.

Sincerely, Theodore

Theodore. My mentor, who'd barely made an appearance these last few days, had decided to slip me a letter and go on his merry way. I ripped it up in anger and slammed the pieces on the bedside table. This was not how I wanted to start my day. For someone who "saved" me, he sure knew how to forget about me. I had come to the conclusion that this whole society was a joke. This place was unorganized, and all the vampires acted like high schoolers during prom week. Dramatic and bitchy. All the rules and regulations made being a dhampir a complete let down. Granted, I hadn't asked for it, but it should have been better than this, right?

Instead of dwelling on the negatives of this life, a good shower might actually lift my spirits back up. I laid out some jeans, undergarments, and a light gray sweater on my bed and made my way to the shower stalls.

The hot water hit my back in the best way, relieving me of tension and loosened the muscles. For a bunch of old guys, they truly had the best showers and amazing plumbing system. In the midst of lathering my hair with shampoo, I heard a couple of voices enter through the door.

"You don't think the Imperium Council would do that, do you?"

"Why not? They've done it before."

I froze as I strained to hear who had entered, shampoo dripping from my hair.

"That's a lot of bodies."

Of course, I was in a female bathroom and the voices were soft and light, so it had to be two females here with me, but who? Why did they sound so familiar?

"This kind hasn't been around for ages, but who's to say they're not trying to make a comeback."

A second shower head turned on beside me, hitting the wall.

"It scares me. I didn't think... reading about it... would actually be true."

Another shower head turned on.

"Relax. They won't touch us. Maybe they'll eat Ivy." Both girls laughed and I knew instantly who they were. Annoyed, and my mood completely ruined, I lathered and rinsed quickly before ducking out of there, towel wrapped securely around me. I just made it past the threshold, when I hit a hard boulder with my shoulder blade. I stumbled back and saw Jackson in jeans and a red flannel long sleeve. *Shit, he looks hot*, I thought. *Shit, I'm still staring like a moron.*

"Sorry," I mumbled.

He smirked, pushing his hair back with his big hands. "Walk much?"

"Don't you have anything better to do?"

"Maybe." A teasing smile hugged the corner of his mouth. I watched his eyes linger on my bare legs to my wet hair on my exposed shoulders. Our eye contact was intense, and I could feel my skin tingle.

"For a guy, you have the worst mood swings."

Jackson laughed and walked by me. I was just about to do the same when he grabbed my bare arm and drew me back. "Ivy." My skin sizzled under his touch. I wondered if he felt it too.

"Do you mind?" I glanced between my arm and his hand.

"Oh, sorry," he loosened his grip, and I back tracked to my bedroom.

"Ivy," he called me again.

I halted at my door, hand on the knob. "Yeah?" I responded over my shoulder.

"Just wanted to make sure you got Theodore's note," he said.

"Yup." I turned the doorknob with such force it slightly cracked under my fingers. *Great.*

I could hear him laughing all the way down the hall. What was he doing over on this side anyway? Then it hit me, Rebecca's room was at the end, the room I'd caught them in...

I huffed a heavy sigh and dried myself off, throwing on the clothes I'd left out and brushing out the knots in my hair. It was then that I noticed the vial of blood on my pillow. Jackson must have placed it there before I collided with him in the hallway. There were times when he left me breathless and others when I wanted to throw myself into oncoming traffic. I shouldn't let him get to me, because let's face it, I was really kidding myself with a possibility of him and I. Pathetic, right? But I was always drawn to him, like a moth to a flame. Desperate for the light, wanting to touch what could hurt me. Maybe that's why he was so half assed with me. Maybe there *was* something he had been denying with himself.

I scooped up the ripped pieces of Theodore's trashy note, opened my window, and tossed it like confetti in the air. A breeze caught the pieces and took them in flight. They swirled a few times before dropping down in a nearby bush.

The business trip charade was getting old. Something was off with Theodore. Even with our first encounter with each other, he'd seemed sketchy from the start. Theodore claimed he saved my life, but why me?

What for? There *had* to be a purpose. I wasn't just some random chick he'd come across and thought "yeah, she's good," no, there had to be more behind it. The memories were clear indicators of that.

My phone chimed underneath my pillow which made me jump out of my inner rambling. I closed the window and grabbed my phone to check my messages. An unknown number appeared on the screen, but the preview message window gave away it was Gypsy. I slid open the phone and read her text.

Gypsy: Gurrrrl, I hounded Jackson for your number. The little shit never told me he gave you a phone! Anywho, I'm inviting you for some outdoor activities today!

I began to type, but back peddled. Was I really in the mood to see people after I unintentionally eavesdropped on Rebecca and Mabel's conversation about me? No. But I also didn't want to disappoint Gypsy either. Maybe they won't be present at the activities.

With a heavy sigh I replied back.

Me: Yeah sure, just give me a few. My hair is still wet.

Within a heartbeat, my phone went off.

Gypsy: You got ten minutes! Meet me out in the back!

I tossed my phone on my bed and finally found a blow dryer hidden underneath the box-spring in a clear storage bin I'd had no idea existed until now. Some combs, curling irons, hair elastics were all tucked neatly inside the storage bin. Another bin, smaller than the first one I dragged out contained lotions, shavings creams, and a bottle of sunscreen. I grabbed the bottle first and squeezed out a good amount to rub over my face. Definitely did not want to take any chances.

I became impatient with blow drying my hair and decided to leave some strands wet since I didn't want to waste any more time and wasn't interested in experiencing the wrath of Gypsy for being late. I tried to find some gloves and a hat, which were surprisingly stored in a mini side closet hidden behind my tall dresser I'd had no idea was there. It went to show how well I knew my surroundings. I guess I should've been concerned by my lack of attention to detail, but I had more important matters to focus on. By the time I reached my bedroom door to leave, my phone was already buzzing with messages from Gypsy. I loved the girl, but she was too impatient for me.

I dashed downstairs and made my way to the outside world.

The autumn air hung heavily around the mansion, and most of the trees had started to become bare. The trail around the house had patches of wet leaves plastered to the forest floor, making it a bit slippery at times to walk on. As I made it to the backyard, I saw most of the dhampirs in a circle, laughing with each other.

I was surprised to see most of the crew—with the exception of Rebecca, Jackson, and Trent. Mabel and Nolan stood close together, and every so often she would exchange soft stares with Gypsy. It was then Gypsy sensed my entrance and she ran over to my side.

"Finally! I was beginning to think you got kidnapped," she laughed.

I rolled my eyes. "Funny."

"Now that you're here, the fall festivities can begin! We're going to rake the leaves, and there is this secret pumpkin patch just over the property line past the forest. We're going to carve pumpkins and have a horror movie marathon!" She grabbed ahold of my jacket and brought me to the circle where a pile of rakes lay in the center. I tried my best to avoid eye contact with Mabel and gave a friendly hello to the twins and Zach.

At one point, Gypsy dragged most of us out to rake leaves and create huge piles to jump in. She called it "bonding" I called it "involuntarily torture." Justin and Tyler would take turns tossing everyone into the pile and I tried my best to run away only to get captured and thrown in, screaming my head off. Zach was the only one standing on the sidelines, watching everyone squeal and catapult into the air. When he looked at me, he nodded in his direction to come join him.

"Having fun," he asked as I jogged over.

"A bit. Don't tell Gypsy, though," I joked.

He smiled and shook his head, laughing. "It's her favorite season." Zach gazed at Gypsy, watching her throw the leaves over her head.

"What happened between you two?" I whispered.

Zach sighed as he shuffled a few leaves with his foot. "She decided to end it, but her reasoning is for her to tell. I'll always love her." He looked over at me with a sad smile. I felt bad for Zach, in some ways, my heart ached for him. Maybe my past self-had been through something similar to what Zach had experienced. Could this explain the nostalgic feeling creeping over me?

"Still no Theodore?" Zach asked, probably to change the subject.

"No. He's been gone since..." I stopped. Zach had no idea about the dead girl and my verdict, and I was just about to blow my cover. Shit.

He looked at me, waiting for an answer.

"I don't remember exactly. All my days tend to blend together now," I lied.

"I heard it was some important business deal. I'm guessing he took Aurora with him because I haven't seen her either."

"Interesting." Now that I think of it, she *had* been missing too. But they were a package deal, so it would only make sense she followed him. By the sound of everyone who mentioned Theodore's absence, it seemed to be normal behavior.

"Did you all get the day off?" I realized that almost all of us were home today.

"Yes and no. Just so happens most of us had today off already." It suddenly occurred to me I never actually asked Zach what his job was.

He looked over at me and began to laugh as if he knew what my follow up question would be. "I help with the stocks. It's boring as hell, but the pay is sweet."

"And everybody else?" I gestured at the group of individuals rolling around in the leaves.

"The twins help with the merchandise. Gypsy is the secretary's assistant at the factory you work at. Nolan helps with the shipment process, also at the factory. Rebecca designs the website, and Mabel helps with surveys to help expand the audience. Her job is easy because she also trains new dhampirs."

"So, Mabel and Jackson train the newcomers?"

"And Trent," he added.

"Trent?"

"Yeah, Mabel, Trent, and Jackson are the three oldest dhampirs. Because of their age and knowledge, they were granted to train all new ones."

"Who's older?"

"Trent. And he's also the most arrogant son of bitch I have ever met. What you saw last night wasn't half of the crap he stirs up."

So, Trent was the oldest, and that wasn't the first time he had acted in that manner. I wanted to ask more questions, but Gypsy came bouncing toward us at top speed.

"Are you ready for the pumpkins?" Her smile was wider than the sun.

"Sure thing!" Zach exclaimed. He winked at me before joining the others. I realized the rest of the crew were already down near the edge of the forest. I was about to walk down to join them, before Gypsy stepped in front of me, blocking my path.

"Are we going to join them—"

"I'm breaking into the library tomorrow morning. Eight am sharp," interrupted Gypsy.

My mind had to backtrack for a second before I realized what she'd said to me. "Wait... really?"

"Yes, and before you ask, no you cannot come, I'm going alone. I finally have a window to grab the books, and word on the street is the council is going to be watching you like a hawk, so it's a no go for you." She bopped the tip of my nose with her finger.

"So?"

"So, you gotta keep a low profile."

I crossed my arms. "If it's in the morning, they're not going to know."

"Oh, they'll know." She wasn't going to budge.

I bit my lip, trying to formulate a rebuttal when she covered my mouth with her hand.

"Ivy, please, just trust me," she begged.

She dropped her hand from my mouth. "Okay." I knew she was right, but it sucked not being a part of the plan.

"Now, let's get those pumpkins!"

We ended up cutting through the forest with the rest of the group, jumping over jagged rocks and ducking under hanging branches. I began to notice how effortlessly everyone talked, even Mabel, who not too long ago, joined in on making fun of me yet now seemed oddly okay with my presence. I watched her look at Gypsy, who was unaware of the attention. Something was nagging at the back of my mind about them. I found it quite interesting as we approached the pumpkin patch how their moves mirrored each other. I remembered what

Zach had said earlier, it was not his place to tell, but when the time was right, I'm sure Gypsy would.

Tyler and Justin were grabbing two pumpkins at a time and putting them against their chests' like a pair of boobs. I laughed when they ran up to me and begged me to touch their "newly implanted titties." Most of us picked out a pumpkin, with the exception of Mabel. It seemed she was too cool to carve pumpkins. I found a small one with a long stem and Gypsy found a huge orange one with green speckles. In the middle of all the laughter and jokes, a piece of my hollow shell was filled. The realization came without notice but told me if this were to be my life forever, then maybe I could make it.

CHAPTER 15

Work dragged on the next day, only because I was anxious as hell to get a text from Gypsy about the books. Did she make it out without getting caught? Was she able to get some at all? The never-ending cycle of questions and anxiety filtered my brain for the rest of my shift until Jackson picked me up. The car ride conversations with him had become sparse. Almost as if we were both struggling to speak to one another. Afraid to say the wrong thing was my problem. Unfortunately, I didn't know what his was. He would also leave me at the front steps to the mansion and disappear somewhere else. Except today, he decided to linger and let me know our training sessions would be changing tomorrow.

"Be prepared for some heavy lifting," he said.

"Are you going to kill me?" I joked.

"That would be too easy," said Jackson.

My wide-eyed gaze made him laugh even harder.

"You don't trust me?" he chuckled.

I don't know. I didn't answer and left him outside to let him think whatever he wanted about my mute response. I wanted to trust him, but there were so many things that had happened so far, it made me question who Jackson really was and what his role was in all of this. It was then, having a conversation in my head and not paying attention, I collided with someone on the top steps. Theodore grabbed me by the shoulders and kept me from toppling backward. I looked at my mentor for the first time in weeks and felt a nasty feeling in the pit of my stomach. Something was off about him. His presence cast a dark cloud of negative energy, almost like death. His eyes sagged from obvious exhaustion, and his complexion looked rough. I had no idea where he had been these last couple of days, but wherever he'd gone, it brought back a stranger. I pulled myself away from his hold, uncomfortable from his touch. This was not the same man who'd changed me.

"Ivy, how are you?" he asked casually. His smile was forced to the point where worried lines wrinkled his forehead.

I was surprised how cool he was acting, given Theodore looked like he'd come from hell and back. "Okay."

"Jackson said you have been progressing well. And Patricia gave me a great review on your work at the factory."

So he had been keeping in touch while he was away, just not with me.

I kept my cool and decided to give him a lame lie to satisfy him. "Yes, I'm enjoying both training and my job at the factory."

"Excellent. Excuse me, but I must be on my way. I have some business to attend to. I'll speak with you soon." Without hesitation, he left me once again with more questions and confusion.

Theodore made me feel disconnected from him. Almost as if he was forcing me out of his circle, but that wasn't going to stop me from finding out the truth. Once Gypsy had access to those books, it was all or nothing from there on out.

I made my way to my bedroom when my phone chimed. A text from Gypsy flashed on my lock screen. *Thank god,* I thought. This was it. I was finally going to get some answers and be one step closer to finding out all the bullshit these people have been keeping from me. Driven by strong emotion, I opened the text to read Gypsy's message.

Gypsy: I'm in my room with the books. Wait five minutes then come over.

Me: Got it.

I watched the clock on my phone tick away the five minutes, eager to get myself in her room. Finally, after the five-minute mark, I took a deep breath and made my way over to Gypsy's bedroom door. Music seemed to be playing inside, just enough to echo through the door frame. I took a deep breath and gave the door a slight knock, hoping she would hear it above all that noise. The door creaked open, and Gypsy stepped out to look around the hallway before pulling me into her room.

"Had to make sure nobody was around," she said.

"Ah," I said.

"Come, sit," Gypsy gestured toward her bed.

The music she played came from a little radio on her nightstand.

"Needed some background noise in case anyone decided to eavesdrop."

I sat down and noticed a theme throughout her room. Posters of boy bands were scattered all over her walls. She had hanging lights on the wall over her dresser and a vanity that was covered in makeup. Her closet was on the opposite side of where mine was placed, and I could see shoes upon shoes piled on the floor inside.

Gypsy could tell I was eyeing her collection when she said, "Online shopping is dangerous."

I snorted. "I can see that."

"Yeah, yeah, yeah," she swatted my arm, "are you ready?"

I nodded eagerly. "Yes."

Gypsy stuck her hand under her pillow and pulled out two thick, brown, leather books, each with a piece of red ribbon hanging from a saved placed inside.

"The first one is our history. The vampiric one. I thought it would be best to start with that one. See if we can trace anything there. Also, it will help you understand our kind better." She handed me one of the brown leather books and opened up to where the ribbon marked one of the pages, "While I was waiting for you to come back from work, I found an interesting page on our council leader," Gypsy pointed to a painting of Artimis in the top right hand corner. In this photo, his hair was longer and wavy, and he looked to be about seventeen, "This painting was made by artist Louis St. Germain in 1318 in Belgium. Artimis said he was from France and remained there until his parents got the okay to cross over." The rest of the page showed family members who had traveled over with him, some died, but not a single picture of Artimis in suit or armor. Did Jackson lie? Or was Artimis the liar?

"Anyway, he's not our main concern, but you can keep that in your room. They don't like us to dig into others' pasts, but they also don't like to tell us what's going on either."

I traced my finger over Artimis' picture, surprised at how innocent he looked there.

"Here's the book I scored. When I saw that symbol Jackson drew, I knew it was familiar. It's from the lost vampire race," Gypsy took the book in my hand and replaced it with another one. The symbol was plastered on the front, engraved in brown leather like the book itself.

"Lost vampire race?" I asked without looking up. The symbol taunted me, reminding me of that day when I first saw the girl dead on the staircase. Her blood oozed from her scalp, driving me into temptation.

"In this book, it describes how a vampire coven was originally created and slaughtered because of the evil it brought," Gypsy explained.

The dream of the girl with the red eyes and veiny face raced through my mind. Her eyes had glowed a brilliant red, and her blue veins pulsated on her porcelain skin. But it was just a dream, and I'd never seen one of those lost vampires before, let alone knew what they looked like. Could it be that it was more than just a dream? Was it a memory? Could I now have memories in my dreams?

"Does it show what the lost vampire race looked like?" I squeaked. Jesus, I needed to calm down.

Gypsy opened the book to where the other red ribbon was marked. Inside, a small section of regular human faces were displayed. Names and dates written under each self-portrait of what appeared to be the lost vampire race. All were stunning and dressed in centuries old clothing. Their features were striking and dangerous. They were from all over the world.

"This is all we have. Not a hundred percent sure if this is what they looked like at all times," said Gypsy.

What struck me the most, was that all seemed to be average citizens at the time in average clothing. As if they'd lived their lives normally but had hidden the creature within. Not that I could tell much, because the portraits were in black and white, but no heavily exposed veins were seen anywhere on their faces. Could it be just a nightmare that I conjured up instead?

"Is there any way I can borrow this one as well?" I asked.

Gypsy bit her lip. "I want to say yes, but this one is from the restricted section."

"I would take the blame if they found out," I told her.

I could tell she was contemplating what I said, when she finally sighed and rolled her eyes at me, "just make sure you have it back to me by the end of the week. The vampire who runs the library is on vacation."

"Thanks!" I got up to leave with both books, ready to dive in on my own when Gypsy's next words caught me off guard.

"I think we should sneak into the basement."

The idea sent an adrenaline rush throughout my whole body. "Can we?" The thought had me excited and a little scared.

"Yes. There's an important dinner coming up with the council. Others will be attending. They'll be too distracted to notice us sneak in and out of the basement," her eyes sparkled with excitement over the plan.

"I'm in."

"Perfect! I'll confirm the time and date for the dinner, and we'll go from there."

"Thank you, Gypsy. For everything."

She smiled and then tossed her pillow at my head. "Now go and study, you goober!"

I laughed my way out of her room, completely at peace with our beautiful friendship.

As I reached my own door, I could feel eyes on the back of my head. The hair on my arms stood up, giving me unwanted goosebumps all over my body. I clenched the books tightly in my arms and waited for whoever was behind me to speak up.

"Hey, you," a deep voice said. It wasn't Zach, or the twins, and it definitely wasn't Jackson.

Do I dare look behind me? I thought. Doubling checking to make sure the book covers weren't exposed, I twisted on my heels slowly, coming face to face with none other than Trent.

CHAPTER 16

"Ivy, is it?" he asked. His lip ring glistened in the hallway light as he flicked it with his tongue. Trent leaned casually on the wall just before the staircase began. I watched his smoldering hazel eyes travel up and down my body before noticing the two big leather-bound books in my arms.

"Whatcha got there?" asked Trent. He placed his hands in his black leather jacket before stalking over to me. My heart thumped loudly against my ribcage, exposing my anxiety to him.

"Just some light reading," I choked.

"Mmmm, light reading," Trent reached over to tap the book and then trailed his finger lightly over my hand. His smile was wicked, and he seemed to be enjoying this little game I desperately didn't want to play.

"I like a girl who reads," confessed Trent. His hand that traced my finger made its way over to my arm, gliding all the way up to my shoulder. My goosebumps from earlier were overly exposed to him now. Why did I choose today to where a tank top? The feeling gave away some type of hidden emotion I'd had no idea would happen between us. I had barely spoken two words to him when we first met, and now he suddenly finds me irresistible? Trent had this overly confident way about him, as if he knew how to capture his prey. The only problem was, he wasn't Jackson.

"Some of us are going out tonight, and I would like to extend the invite," he cooed. His finger tickled the tip of my shoulder.

"Are w... we... allowed to?" I stuttered.

"It's tradition, we sneak out. Don't worry, we won't get caught," he leaned in to whisper the last sentence in my ear. His breath fanned my neck, which had me feeling hot in my groin.

My head was spinning from his close proximity to my face. He leaned back slightly, inches away from my trembling lips. *What the fuck was wrong with me?* I thought. *Was being horny part of the vampire world?* Or was I desperate for some kind of intimate action because Jackson and I would never be, and that bothered me too much to admit.

"I don't know..."

"It will be fun. We meet tonight at ten in the foyer," his finger made its way to my face, along my cheek, and then finally brushed my lower lip.

"Wow, Trent, can you hide your boner any better?"

His finger released my bottom lip, "Now, Rebecca, it's rude to intrude on someone's private conversation."

I peeked around his body to see Rebecca's cocky smirk. If anything, this would be another humiliating story she would pass around to everyone.

"Why am I not surprised to see you, Ivy," she said sweetly.

Anger welled up inside me. I pushed past Trent and got right in front of Rebecca's face. "Can you, for once, just shut the fuck up?"

Shocked spread from her eyes to mouth as her jaw dropped twenty feet. Rebecca recovered quickly and stood up straight, trying to seem taller than me.

"Better watch yourself." Her shoulder whacked hard against mine before she made her way to her room. I massaged my shoulder, trying to relieve some of the pressure, when Trent came up behind me and grabbed my waist.

"I hope you can make it tonight," his tongue glazed over my neck, making me jump. He released his hold on me and left without another word.

Between Trent's overly horny demeanor and Rebecca's snarky comment, I was ready to dig my own grave and gladly jump in to never been seen again.

A door creaked open to my right and Gypsy's head popped out. "So, are we going?"

Nighttime rolled around and Gypsy had caked my entire face with almost every product on her vanity. It felt like over a hundred dollars' worth of product were dabbed, smeared, and plastered on every crevasse, hiding imperfections and accentuating my features. When I got to look at the final result, I didn't recognize the girl in the mirror. Her eyes were wide but sexy from the smoky eye. Her lips were full and luscious from the crimson red lipstick. Everything about this girl, from her curled hair to pouty mouth, screamed sexy. And it made me feel insecure.

"You like it?" asked Gypsy. She sprayed a few more strains of hairspray on some curls before she stepped back.

"It's different," I said.

"But, good different?"

"You did a wonderful job, really. Just not used to this yet." I wonder if my past self-enjoyed these moments. If I was into all this girly stuff.

She smiled and squeezed my shoulder. "Now, it's time to pick an outfit!"

Gypsy skipped over to her overflowing closet and picked out a few dresses in a variety of colors. She laid each one out on her bed so she could show me the design better. "Since we went with a red lip, I think either this black number or red one should really top off the look."

I held up the black and red ones and cringed. Both had deep V-neck cuts and the black one had a sheer lining from the waist down to the shins. The red seemed to be safer, but I was still uncomfortable with the idea of my boobs hanging out.

"The red one," I said.

"Ooo! Good choice!" she clapped her hands together, smiling from ear to ear.

I undressed as Gypsy finished her make-up, dark eyes like mine with a nude lip instead of red. She grabbed an electric blue, skin-tight dress with silver heels. After a few attempts of shimmying the dress over my thighs, I made sure my breasts were securely in place behind the extra padding in the cup region and smoothed out any wrinkles.

"Pick any heels you want. Next paycheck, we're going shopping for you to get some club clothes," she said.

I dug through the pile and found some nude, short inch heels with a simple strap that went around the ankles. Gypsy was done by the time I put on both heels, and I was in awe of my best friend. Her caramel skin against the electric blue was mesmerizing and the silver heels really complimented her long legs. Any runway model would kill to have a body like hers.

"Oh my god, Ivy. You look incredible!" she squealed.

I smile awkwardly. "I don't know, compared to you. Gypsy, you look stunning."

She twirled around a few times in her dress to show me all angles. "Let's take a picture!"

Gypsy snagged her phone hidden underneath her pillow and motioned for me to stand by her. She held out the phone at arms-length and had me do multiple selfies with different faces.

"Definitely printing these out later," she mused.

I flattened the front of my dress one more time, making sure I didn't resemble an overripe apple when I stepped out of Gypsy's room. I was nervous, I couldn't deny that. Going out for the first time without Jackson gave me millions of butterflies, and I almost wanted to puke. But with Gypsy there, I was sure I could handle it. I hoped.

"Here, I snagged this from Jackson earlier. He had a few errands to run, and he wanted me to give you this." Gypsy handed me a vial of blood from her mini, matching, silver purse.

"Thanks." As lady-like as I could be, I downed my entire meal in one gulp. The blood rushed through my body, leaving me on an all-time high. I licked the corner of my mouth, trying to capture whatever I missed from the vial. I noticed the blood was thicker and more potent than the last batch. I wondered if Jackson finally changed my formula so I wouldn't rip peoples' heads off.

"Ready?" asked Gypsy.

"Ready," I echoed. Gypsy took out her own vial and swigged it down in one motion. It was the first time I had seen anyone else drink blood besides myself. She wiped her mouth with the back of her hand and led the way to the foyer. Walking in heels was a project, and finding my balance was even more of a hassle, but I somehow managed not to fall on my ass when I trekked down the staircase. When we got to the last step, we noticed almost everyone was decked out in club clothing. From black skinny jeans, to leather jackets, and tight dresses, all were ready for a night out on the town. The smell of cologne and cheap perfume made a thick cloud around us.

Gypsy bubbled with excitement next to me. "This is going to be a fun night. I can tell."

Trent emerged from the dhampir rec room with slicked back hair, his famous leather jacket, and all black jeans and tee. He caught sight of me next to Gypsy and gave me a playful wink. I blushed and averted my eyes somewhere else. *What is wrong with you*, I thought. *You can't trust him.*

"Ladies and gentlemen, the Uber has arrived," he announced.

Zach, the twins, Mabel, Gypsy, and Nolan led the way outside to the waiting vehicle. I followed just shortly behind, when Rebecca yanked me back to her.

"Wouldn't it be the icing on the cake to let Jackson know what a little sneak you are?" she threatened.

I tugged my arm out of her grasp. "Don't you have anything better to do than to pick on me?"

"Now why would I do that? You're just so easy to make fun of. I can't wait to tell Jackson where you've been tonight," she cackled.

Rebecca strutted out in knee-high, black boots, white, sheer blouse, and mini skirt, making it known she wasn't playing around.

Trent sneaked up beside me and grabbed my hand.

"Don't let the wicked witch of the west get to you," he murmured. Trent's fingers were tightly laced with mine as he stroked my thumb with his. The feeling gave me small flips to my stomach, but it didn't compare to Jackson's touch. Not even close.

Trent escorted me to the Uber, a black minivan with bright lights lit up the whole driveway. He slid the door out, and I climbed in the back, taking an empty seat next to Gypsy. She could tell I was not happy when she reached over to squeeze my hand.

"What happened?" she asked in a hushed voice.

"Rebecca threatened to expose me tonight," I whispered back.

"Yeah and ruin it for the rest of us, including herself? She's a fake."

I laughed and leaned my head on Gypsy's shoulder. "What would I do without you?"

"Your fashion sense would be horrid."

The club was chaotic, in the best way. Music was blaring from all corners with some heavy techno beat I didn't recognize but couldn't help but bop too. Everyone around us had dressed in provocative club attire, and some already begun making out with strangers. Our group migrated toward the bar first, laughing as Trent used a fake I.D. to order all of us drinks. Since we couldn't compel the bartender like a regular vampire, we had to do it the old fashion way. Trent slid a vibrant pink drink my way, giving me his famous wink in the process. I smiled back and took a tiny sip, preparing myself for an overabundance of alcohol to invade my taste buds. To my surprise, the drink was incredibly fruity, and it had masked whatever type of vodka that was mixed in. Really enjoying myself now, I chugged the first drink without hesitation.

"Ooo yes, girl!" cheered Gypsy.

"Who knew the newbie could drink," said Tyler as he came over to give me a high-five.

Our hands connected with a loud smack and I burst out in giggles. "I'm tired of being safe. I'm ready to party!"

"Hell yeah!" cheered Justin.

Trent slid me another drink, and we all clinked our glasses together, toasting to friends and the dhampir life. Once I was done with the second, Gypsy grabbed my hands and led me straight onto the dance floor. Tyler and Justin followed in pursuit, taking up center stage to show off their moves. The heavy beat changed tempo to another song, a bit slower but just enough to dance solo too. I swayed my hips to the beat, getting lost in the moment. My mind hadn't felt this clear since the day I woke up and discovered my fate as a dhampir. All the stress and unwanted emotions exited from my body. Tyler and Justin found two girls to dance with, or should I say grind with. For the first time in the past few songs, I noticed Gypsy had disappeared from my side. In a panic, I scanned the dance floor, searching for that mop of curly dark hair, when I spotted her in the corner with Mabel, locking lips. It all made sense after that. The comment Zach had made earlier. The way Mabel looked at Gypsy and vice versa. But why Mabel? She was Rebecca's right hand man and enjoyed making fun of me just as much. I awkwardly stumbled my way back over to the bar where Trent, Zach, and unfortunately Rebecca lounged against. Trent could tell I needed a drink, but before I could ask for water, he slid over another vibrant pink drink.

"I'm cutting myself off early," I yelled over the music.

He shook his head no and pushed the drink against my hands. *You know what? Fuck it.*

In a greedy manner, I grabbed the beverage from the counter and finished it off with just one swig. I slammed the glass back down and drunkenly headed back onto the dance floor, bumping against everyone else in the crowd on my way there. Trent's laugh bounced between the beat of the music, but I didn't care enough to turn around.

Song after song, I swayed and rocked my hips, feeling the music take control. It wasn't until halfway through the second chorus when hands began to travel around my waist. I was too preoccupied with my own moves to even care who took the lead. My hips grinded hard against someone, and I was really hoping Trent had finally made his way to me. Out of curiosity and hoping it was him, I turned around to find another guy, a stranger, dancing with me. He was incredibly good looking with dark eyes and hair, and he smelled like expensive colon. The disappointment sizzled out when he reached for both my hands to place on his chest, still keeping a firm grip on my waist. I wasn't going to lie, I really enjoyed the attention he gave me. Our foreheads pressed together as we danced in sync with the beat. Every movement I made, he would mirror, and it left me craving more. Without warning, he kissed me, and I hungrily kissed back. We made out hard on the dance floor, and I was secretly wishing Trent was watching. My hands traveled all over his body, into his hair where I pulled when he bit my lower lip. The heat from the kiss had me lost and unaware of all the moaning being produced deep in my throat.

"You're so sexy," he moaned against my lips.

I gripped his neck and pulled him in for another kiss, desperate for more and not interested in talking, when my hand became covered in warm liquid. I pulled back, lifting my hand, trying to see under the club lights what I touched, when the smell hit me.

It dripped down my palm, creating a trail onto my forearm. All around me, the people and the music became muffled. A sharp ring penetrated my eardrums, and I was having a hard time focusing on my breathing. My vision became hazy as I tried to search for my friends. In the corner of the bar, Trent locked eyes with me, lifted his glass, and winked. As if a light switch came on, I realized what Trent did, but it was too late. I was hungry. The innocent man before me smiled drunkenly, not realizing his fate was sealed the minute he began to dance with me. There was no way I could control what I was about to do next. I leaned in and grazed my tongue lightly on his wound. That's when the blood came at a constant flow. The taste exploded on my tongue and without a second thought, I covered the wound with my mouth and began to suck out the blood. I latched my body to his, trying to drain every ounce as quickly as I could before I got caught.

"Ooo, baby, that feels so good," he moaned. His large hand cupped my ass, positioning me into a better spot, squeezing around my cheek, and I continued to suck and lick like an animal. All around me was white noise compared to the personal bubble of just us two caught in a sexual frenzy.

I was just about to sink my teeth in deeper, testing to see if I could produce a bigger flow, when another pair of hands yanked me away from his neck.

"Alright, you're fucking done. Let's go."

Jackson. Everything came crashing down at once. I was on overdrive with my senses, when I knocked Jackson down on his ass. The crowd circled around us, and I became the center of attention. Jackson shot right up and grabbed me from behind, carrying me through the crowd and out to the cool air.

"Let go of me!" I struggled against his strong hold. My legs kicked forward, trying to loosen his grip.

"No." he said firmly.

Jackson carried me all the way to his black truck down the street from the club and forced me into the passenger seat. About two seconds later, he appeared on the driver's side and got in. The locks on all the doors clicked and he sped off down the road, maneuvering through traffic like a maniac.

"Was that really necessary?" I snapped.

"You're kidding me, right? You almost outed the entire dhampir race, including vampire. And would you put your seatbelt on!" he shouted.

I fumbled with the clip on the seatbelt and finally managed to snap it into place. "There! Happy?"

"No, Ivy, I'm not fucking happy."

"How is this my fault?"

"It's not, it's mine."

"What?"

Jackson gripped the steering wheel and squinted at the road ahead. "I should've known better when Trent came into my room today to make peace about the patrols, that he would go behind my back and get revenge," he ran his long fingers through his hair and took a deep breath, "I had a vial of blood set out for you with the new formula, and after our truce, Trent offered to take it to you..."

"But Gypsy gave it to me," I interrupted.

"Yes, but I ran into Gypsy before you two were getting ready to go out, and she told me she already got your blood ready to go. Shortly after you left, it all clicked together," he finished.

It explained the blood thickness and the taste was sweeter. "So, Trent swapped vials."

He nodded. "Exactly."

I rested my head on the window, my temples throbbing from tonight's rush. "Who the hell made this stupid night out a tradition anyway?"

"Me."

CHAPTER 17

The next morning, I wished for death. My head was pounding profusely, and a few times already, I'd had to make a trip to the bathroom to dry-heave in the toilet. No dhampir warned me of the after-effects from too much alcohol intake, but my guess was, because I was still half human, I would still be affected by it. I called out of work and gave them an elaborate excuse of it being food poisoning, and I might be out for another day. Earl, sweet Earl, told me to get better soon because a new shipment was coming in for the wine, and he was excited for everyone to taste. After that conversation, I was back over the toilet heaving.

Last night's events replayed over and over in my head. Jackson was pissed when we got into the house and told me he was going to have a nice chat with Trent. I hadn't heard from either since. Gypsy was missing in action, and if my guess was correct, I think she was occupied in someone else's bed. I'd have to score the details later.

Coming back from the bathroom after my fiftieth trip over the toilet, Rebecca came strutting my way with a nasty smirk on her face.

"For a blood addict, you hold your liquor like a bitch," sneered Rebecca.

I flipped her off to show her I wasn't in a good mood to deal with her high school antics and hid in my room for the rest of the evening. It was later in the evening when a soft knock rippled on my door.

"Yes?" I said weakly.

The door creaked open to Zach's facing peering inside. The light behind him from the hallway came through and made my eyes water.

"Ahhhh! Please shut the door," I whined.

He chuckled. "Damn, you went down hard."

A heavy weight sagged at the end of my bed. I peeked from under the covers and saw Zach smiling like a goofball. He waved a vial of blood at me and I almost keeled over onto my bedroom floor.

"Mixing strong alcohol and consuming a lot of blood is not the best combo," he joked.

"No shit," I croaked.

"I heard what happened," he mumbled.

"Great," I groaned.

Zach shifted on the end of my bed and I could feel him leaning over me. "Ivy, you need to drink. The new formula is a part of it now, and it'll help you."

I groaned, my stomach curdling at the thought.

"Ivvyyyyy."

I put my palm facing up out from the covers and felt the cold vial touch me. Slithering it back in like a snake, I shakily uncorked the top and plugging my nose, swallowed the blood. At first, I wanted to projectile vomit everywhere, but after a couple of minutes, the blood settled in and waved away my queasy stomach. My head still had a slight touch of tenderness, but I was eighty-five percent better than where I first began.

"Thanks," I smiled.

"Dr. Zach knows everything," he said.

The remnants of last night came to the front part of my mind and the image of Gypsy and Mabel replayed over and over. I looked at Zach and finally understood everything, even after all of it, he still loved her and respected her decision. I made the choice to keep what I'd witnessed to myself and patted his hand.

"What's that for?" asked Zach.

"For being a good friend," I replied.

His smile radiated throughout the room. "Well, I gotta get back to my pool game with the twins. Somehow, I'm kicking their ass." Zach gave me a quick side hug and exited the room.

I was alone again, but this time, I felt more myself. The blood really did help, surprisingly, and the spins had disappeared along with the sudden urge to puke. I'd admit, I was a coward to face everyone in the rec room because of my actions last night, but this was all Trent's fault. I had trusted him, and it was stupid of me to do so. He made me feel important and a little sexy. How stupid of me to believe so quickly because of a few little comments and touches.

I got up to stretch, finally having some sort of strength to stand on my own two feet for more than a minute, and made my way over to my window. The stars shone brightly, and the moon was half quarter and glowing just above the forest line. All the clouds were vacant in the sky tonight, which gave the moon a chance to rule over the horizon on its own. To be a bird and fly through that scenery would be worthwhile—to experience everything from its point of view. Sadness washed over me like a tidal wave, and I was suddenly wishing I could be anywhere but there. A few tears trickled down my face, overwhelmed from everything, when a hand touched my shoulder.

I jumped to the side with a yelp escaping from my mouth and noticed Trent standing in front of me.

"Uh, what are you doing here?' I demanded.

"I heard you crying and wanted to make sure you were alright," he said innocently.

Was I being that loud? "Thanks, but I'm okay now."

Hurt crossed his face, and I knew right then and there, he wasn't going to leave. "Are you mad at me?"

"I mean, you gave Gypsy the wrong vial and got me incredibly drunk, then it escalated into me feeding on a poor, innocent guy, which might I add you brought him over to me wounded, so yeah, I kind of am," I huffed.

Trent started laughing. "I sent him over. I knew you needed a stronger buzz to get the night going the way you truly wanted it too. Don't tell me you weren't having fun?"

Realization froze me into place. "What?" He really did plan this whole charade out.

Trent inched his way over to where I stood. "Ivy, it's okay. We all crave attention."

Was he fucking serious? "That's not who I am."

"Oh, but it is." Trent finally reached me and brushed a strand of my hair away from my face.

I flinched. "Trent..."

"Shh... it's okay, baby," he cupped his hand on my cheek and began to lean in. I was paralyzed. Putty, because I knew I was weak. The dangerous part of him sent my skin aflame, and I didn't want to pull away. Why didn't I want to pull away?

"What the fuck is going on here."

Both of us froze. Standing in the doorway was Jackson with a pissed off look on his face.

"Do you mind?" snapped Trent.

"Yeah, I fucking do," Jackson shot back.

I stepped back from Trent's hand and stepped back against the wall, waiting for the scene to mellow out.

"Are you jealous, Jackson?" assumed Trent.

Jackson stepped into my room, his face completely red with anger. "Get away from her. You've done enough damage." His arms flexed as if he was ready to strike.

"Nah, I think I'll stay right here. Besides, Ivy invited me over." Trent looked over at me and winked.

"Wait... Jackson..." I had no clue why I was trying to defend myself, when I was just about to kiss Trent two minutes ago.

He ignored me, and I couldn't react fast enough. Jackson planted a right hook across Trent's cheek. He stumbled back a bit and spit some blood on the floor. The testosterone level was at an all-time high in my bedroom, and it needed to end. Now.

"Guys! Please!" I begged, coming in between them.

"Don't worry about me, baby. Jackson is just jealous." Trent leaned down without warning and planted a fat, bloody kiss on my lips. After a couple of awkward minutes, Trent released me and stormed out of the room, leaving Jackson and I finally making eye contact with one another.

"Jackson..." I stopped. Afraid to say anymore. His face was expressionless, as if he was hiding under a mask.

He looked down at me like I was a small child, ready to be punished for disobeying.

"Just wanted to let you know, tomorrow evening we will be working out in the gym, and to meet me outside on the front steps when the sun hides behind the clouds" his voice was cold.

All I could do was nod without crying. He accepted my response and exited himself from my room, shutting the door roughly behind him.

I fell to my knees and began to sob. This was far from my fault, but I felt like I should be the one to blame. I'm weak, a coward, and to be quite frank, an absolute dumbass. I let Trent get under my skin, and for that, paid the price of losing Jackson's trust. It was clear as day all over his face. He truly believed I'd invited Trent over to my room. Even though I hadn't, he walked in on our almost kiss and caught me red handed. I wiped my mouth of the blood that lingered on my lips from Trent's kiss, and staggered into my bed, defeated. *I'm a poor excuse for a dhampir,* I thought. My morals were all over the place. I grabbed my phone and wiped my tears, ready to text Gypsy with the details.

Me: Trent kissed me.

I locked my phone and waited for a reply.

About thirty minutes went by, and still no word from Gypsy. Usually, she would be all over this gossip, but the silence from her was deafening. It was wrong to keep sleeping, but I didn't want to be awake anymore. My eyes were puffy and sore from obnoxiously crying for the past two hours. Did I feel any better? No. Was I going to continue with my shenanigans? Maybe. Trent made me feel... sexy, but Jackson made me feel alive. Two men, both with personal issues, add them together and I had a toxic love triangle-ish.

Closing the curtain and shutting off the lights, I crawled back into bed and under the warm covers. Sleep welcomed me in a warm embrace—protection from the world's demons.

CHAPTER 18

I awoke in a cold sweat, the sound of a female's scream echoed throughout the mansion. Panic rose in the back of my throat as I made my way into the hallway. Most of us emerged from our rooms, looking around frantically, trying to find the source of the scream. Another shrill yelp followed by a cry was heard at the bottom of the stairs toward the foyer. There, hunched over, was Gypsy, sobbing uncontrollably. Not a second thought ran through my mind when I hurried down the stairs to reach her. I wrapped my arms protectively around her and smoothed out her damp hair.

"Gypsy," I mused.

She shook with each breath to inhale from her crying. "No, no, no."

The room around us became crowded with the others, all watching us.

"Gypsy," I repeated softly.

She turned to me so fast I didn't recognize her at first. Gypsy's eyes glowed a familiar red, and her veins pulsated all over her delicate face, "*NO!*"

I jolted forward, only this time, I was aware of being awake. My heart thumped aggressively inside my chest. Sometime between when I had first passed out to now, a dream had crept into my slumber. And here I'd thought I was going to get some actual rest. I turned over onto my side and noticed my screen on my phone lit up. A text from Gypsy.

Gypsy: SHUT THE FUCK UP! I'm coming by your room at 8. The council is having a dinner party with the other guests around 7:30. Should be enough time to sneak in and out of the basement. Can't wait to hear about Trent's kiss! ;)

Yikes. Now I definitely regretted telling her. It was four in the morning, and part of me wanted to avoid going back to sleep. Making a quick decision, I tiptoed out of my room, down the stairs, and out the front door. If I remember correctly, the path to the sanctuary Jackson had taken me to would be on the trail to the right in the back. I followed by memory, stepping over wet leaves and scattered rocks. Like riding a bike, the trail revealed itself to me when I veered right. The smell of sap and pine filled my lungs, and the cool, crisp, autumn air bit at my nose and cheeks. I was glad I'd worn pants and a long sleeve shirt to bed, I admired the oil lamps on the path. They flickered and danced, making the leaves dance with them. Finally, I reached the end of the path and cozied up on the bench, listening to the waterfall trickle through the rocks. The only place I could find peace, stillness, and to shut off my loud thoughts. This sanctuary was clarity. I didn't need Jackson to go there, but part of me wished he was with me. It was the only place I knew that revealed Jackson's true self. His true self I would probably never see again. What a mess I'd created because I had found one moment of pure bliss and selfishness. I let Trent weasel his way under my skin only to manipulate me. Instead, it led to fights, drama, and Jackson planting a swift punch at Trent's face. Only because I couldn't accept the fact that he didn't want me. So, I thrived on someone else's attention. Trent's attention. He was right. I am that type of girl to crave it. How childish and stupid am I? *Immensely*, I thought.

Every sound in this sanctuary, gave me some type of comfort. It was just enough to have me doze off, completely unbothered.

"Ivy?"

"Oh shit, sorry!" I jumped up and wiped the drool from my mouth, embarrassed. It drenched my sleeve on my shirt and pieces of my hair. How cute.

"What are you doing out here?" asked Jackson.

"Uh... couldn't sleep. You?"

"Patrolling."

Oh. He looked down at me, eyes filled with some emotion. Jackson held out his hand for me to take. I obliged and rose from the bench, stiff and a little sore.

"How long was I asleep for?" I asked.

"It's four-thirty in the morning, so you tell me."

"Thirty minutes." But it felt like hours.

"I think it's best if you head back now."

He crossed his arms and nodded his head to the direction behind me. I didn't want to argue, it would be stupid of me to stay and try. Jackson waited until I found my will to walk and left the area. He had a guard up with me now. I could feel it, and he'd built the structure himself. I wanted to apologize, but I had no idea where to begin. Tiptoeing back inside, I climbed the stairs two at a time and went back to bed, again.

The clock ticked loudly throughout the mansion, as I made my way into Gypsy's room. Her and I had the whole plan mapped out. She stole a layout from the librarian's desk to help execute it. Gypsy knew and circled where each security camera was placed and how to enter the control room to wipe them from the circuit. After that, Gypsy would stand guard at the bottom of the basement stairs, keeping an eye on the door. It would be my job to uncover the bodies and examine them. We both drank from our vials and prepared to leave her room. I mentally made a list and checked off all the things I might encounter and how to handle it. Being scared shitless was putting it lightly.

"Now, before we go, I need to ask you one more time," she said.

"Yeah?"

"Did Jackson really punch Trent in the face?"

"Okay, I'm leaving without you."

We'd spent the first hour of prepping discussing the scene with Trent and Jackson and how men still didn't mature even as dhampirs. Gypsy found it comical that Jackson had given Trent the good one-two and was solely convinced he'd done it out of jealousy and not because Trent tricked me.

"Alright! Fine! I'm shutting up now. Let's go," said Gypsy.

We tried to walk as casually as we could through the halls, reminding ourselves the cameras were still on us until we got into the control room. Gypsy led the way, heading through weird side doors in the west wing. Rooms I had no idea existed led to another and another. It became a never-ending maze of rooms and doors. Finally, we stopped outside a small room with a metal door at the end of the hallway. Gypsy motioned me to move forward with her until we approached it.

"This is it. I just need a few minutes. You wait here in case anyone decides to show up," she instructed.

Gypsy pulled out a white key card and swiped it through the locked panel. She slipped in and shut the door tightly behind her.

Strange, vampires still needed tight security to protect their things. I went through each step of the plan while guarding the door, when Gypsy finally emerged from inside.

"All set. Now if we backtrack a few rooms, there's a quicker way to get to the basement."

We hurried back through the maze. It wasn't until Gypsy stopped short, and I slammed into her, that she realized we'd gone too far.

"Dammit," she hissed.

"What do we do now?" I asked.

"I wanted to avoid this, but we're gonna have to use the main entrance to the basement," sighed Gypsy.

We dashed as quietly as we could back through the main foyer. From there, we started from the beginning, only this time, we found the kitchen. White tiles and stainless appliances covered the entire space. A beautiful chandelier hung in the center, and brown wooden stools went around the center island. The countertops were white marble, and the cabinets had been painted a dark gray. Gypsy went around the island and opened up a door on the far left.

"Down here," she said.

I gulped. Adrenaline kicked in as we descended into the cold basement. When we reached the bottom, Gypsy planted herself in position and encouraged me to keep going. Each step I took, I became more aware of what I was about to do. In the back corner of the basement, four metal beds held four bodies covered in white sheets. My heart thumped, rattling my ribcage. I walked closer to the display of bodies, anxiety trailing behind me. When I reached them, the smell of decay tickled my nose. I held my breath and tried not to gag, praying the bodies hadn't decomposed enough to destroy any evidence. I decided to try the first sheet. It seemed to smell the least fowl, and my guess was, it had to be the girl I had seen on the front steps. With a shaky hand, I reached forward and flipped back the white sheet. Laying in front of me was a girl, the girl, placed on her stomach. Her hair fanned the metal bed and her back, hiding the mark. I breathed in and out to center myself and swiped her hair away. Jackson was right. The mark was exactly as he'd described and drawn for me. It was quite exquisite. The lines from the heart down to the teardrop and back up through it were much thicker. Tempted to touch, I had my fingertips graze the mark. The coldness made me shiver, and then my vision became blurred.

I was once again seeing through the eyes of my younger self. An older gentleman—and me sitting on his lap. He hummed a familiar tune and rubbed my back and we rocked in the chair to the melody. I smiled at the older man just as he smiled back at me. My petite hands reached forward and traced a familiar marking on his forearm.

"Grandpa, what is this?" I asked.

"I'll tell you soon, my sweet pea. But for now, let's enjoy our time together," he said.

The memory fizzled out, and I stood there, my fingers still touching the corpse. I pulled back and covered it back up with the sheet. Without thinking, I ripped off the other three sheets, revealing each body of the past victims. All were female with similar features, wavy dark hair, small physique and had the same marking in the exact spot on the back of the neck. *What does this mean?* I thought. *Who did this and why?*

I heard footsteps rushing forward as Gypsy caught up to me and started to pull me with her in the opposite direction.

"What's wrong?" I asked.

"The Butler is coming! I forgot the cooler for the blood bags is down here!"

"Is there another way out?!"

"Yes! Now let's go!"

"Wait! The bodies! I have to cover them up again!" Throwing each sheet on as best I could, I caught up to Gypsy in the center of the basement.

We ran further into the basement to stop at a wall with a small window a few feet above. Deja vu kicked in, and I was suddenly reliving my first nightmare—sans the guy and his gun and the crazy lady. Gypsy snagged a small stepstool underneath one of the shelves and hoisted herself up onto the window ledge. She unlatched the lock and pushed herself up and through effortlessly. I stepped up next and gripped the ledge, shaking, trying to lift myself. Gypsy poked back in and extended both her hands to pull me through. With a little more effort, I finally slithered right out and on to the wet grass.

"Did you see?" she asked out of breath.

"Just enough," I replied. The vision still embedded in my brain.

"Good, let's go."

CHAPTER 19

We made it back to our rooms unscathed, my adrenaline rush subsiding when I collapsed dramatically on my bed. Gypsy thought it was best to be separated for the night and to discuss the findings in the early hours so nobody would suspect it was us two sneaking around. In the meantime, I was going to do some digging on my own. I retrieved the notebook Jackson had left in my room a couple of weeks ago and a pen I'd scored from the rec room to begin my web. I started from my first memory, retracing each step as accurately as I could. I began in the middle, writing down "dog." I circled it and then drew a line up to the Christmas memory. Next, I connected another web to the symbol and the older man who represented it. After that, I wrote downward bubbles to each of the three main ones, adding detail and personal thoughts. The conclusion I came to was—the common factor was me, obviously. Then, the people involved and what they meant to me. The last memory was a dead giveaway, seeing as I had called the gentleman grandpa. My other two guesses followed with the Christmas memory, both adults had to be my parents. The resemblance I carried with that woman was undeniable. The boy also had strikingly similar features, but I was sort of half and half on that. When it came to my first memory, the dog had to be a family dog, but he was absent in the Christmas one. There was one thing left to confirm about the older gentleman, and I it gave me unwanted chills.

Underneath my pillow, I snagged the lost vampire race book and flipped through until I got to the gallery portion of the vampires involved. I scanned up and down, shifting through dates, names, and, more importantly, faces. When I reached the 90s, I came to a staggering halt at the bottom right hand corner. A man, so familiar, I felt like I was back in that memory. Underneath his photo read, *Kaspar Lane, birth 1939 in Georgetown*. His death year was marked 1997. The only way to find out if this was true—I needed to confirm my own birthday and age. Two things I had no idea where to find.

I turned the page and began a new outline of notes, all surrounded by the mark. I'd come to the conclusion that so far, all the targets were female with similar features. The mark was always placed at the back of their necks. If I was on the right path, I could assume the males bore the mark on their right forearm, but I wasn't a hundred percent sure. My supposed grandfather had one of his own, but why was he so old? People of our kind are usually beautiful, from what I seen so far, but he did not fall in the young category. I made a special section for Kapser Lane, to remind myself to do more digging on him.

Then there was the dream I'd had of the girl with the red eyes and veiny face. What if a memory had turned into a dream? At this point, anything could be possible. I jotted down the dream and made parallels to the girl in the basement. Now that I thought about it, what if that was how the lost vampire race... transformed... when they fed? Could it be possible? What if they were never lost to begin with? The possibilities swirled around in my head like a merry-go-round. I put the notebook down and rubbed my temples, trying to process all the details that I'd compiled together. So far, my memories seemed to be the common denominator. Somewhere, there was a fine line that could explain everything. I just needed to connect it all, but I didn't know how.

Eventually, I gave up and realized that I could possibly be going insane, and everything was all in my head. Maybe something went wrong in the process of my transformation, and I was just having a psychotic break. For all I knew, this could be a dream within a dream, and I was in a coma inside a fancy hospital. I gathered up all my materials and shoved them underneath my mattress. Just then, my phone went off. A text from Jackson lit up my screen and so did another from an unknown number. I ignored the message from Jackson and clicked on the unknown number.

14012669570: Hey, it's Trent :)

My heart crashed against my ribcage. How did he get my number?

Me: Hey

I quickly went into my contacts and added him to my list.

Trent: Look out your window.

Confused, I got up and did exactly as he said. There, in the middle of the backyard, Trent sat on a checkered blanket with a picnic basket and a few candles lit, circled around him. He waved from his position and I waved back. My phone vibrated again in my hands.

Trent: Come here.

I backed away from the window and contemplated if I should. Jackson would be furious and most likely try to punch Trent again. On the other hand, I was only Jackson's trainee and nothing more. Trent was also responsible for my almost outing of the dhampir/vampire race, but deep inside I knew he was right. I needed some release, and I wanted it badly. Trent was dangerous, mysterious, and sexy. What was the harm in being with someone who wasn't going to hesitate to bite the bullet? I'd told myself I wouldn't put myself in these situations with Trent, but I didn't care anymore. Without a second thought, I changed my clothes and got myself outside faster than a bunny jacked up on steroids.

Trent could see me around the corner before I saw him, and he stood up, smiling like a goofball. I half jogged over to him, eager for him to explain.

"Ahh, there you are!" he said.

"What's all this?" I observed his work. Five candles made a cute little circle around the picnic he'd set up.

"Just wanted to make good on our date."

"Wait, hold up. When did I say yes to a date? And when did you ask?"

"Right now, and I can tell in your eyes you want to say yes."

The intensity from his stare made me hot. Trent held out his hand for me, and I took it, unsure of where the night could lead to, but a part of me wanted to find out.

Trent guided me to step over the candles and had me sit right across from him on the blanket. A cool breeze whisked its way in between us, and I was silently thanking myself I wore a sweatshirt and pants. He unclipped the clasp on the basket and pulled out a bottle of wine and some bread and weirdly shaped cheeses.

"Human food," I commented.

"They're having a buffet in the dining room tonight, so I scored some of the stuff," he said.

"I haven't had human food since..." I trailed off.

"Since your transformation? Yeah, can't tell you it tastes the same, because we don't remember, but it's good."

Trent made a platter and placed it in the center, then pulled out two wine glasses and poured us some, handing one glass to me.

"Cheers," he said, clinking my glass with his.

I smiled and took a sip, surprised to find it was the wine the factory made.

"Stealing merchandise too?" I teased.

He chuckled and took another swig from his wine glass. "The house is filled with this stuff. Very convenient."

I took a piece of bread and cheese and popped it into my mouth. It tasted good, but slightly off on my taste buds. Human food was definitely tolerable, but not my first choice. Another sip of my wine, and Trent pulled out some fruit in a small bowl. He then proceeded to take out napkins and small dishes, handing one to me and kept the other. I watched as he split up the fruit, which contained strawberries and raspberries.

"You really know how to pull out all the stops, don't you?" I said.

"Only for special people like you, Ivy." His eyes melted into mine, causing me to blush an ugly shade of red.

Trent took one strawberry and leaned forward to my mouth. I obliged and opened wide as he placed the juicy strawberry in between my lips. He watched me intensely as I took a big bite. It was sweet, just like this moment between us. I gazed at Trent like he was the north star. Just an hour ago, I had refused to see him again, now I was caught like a deer in headlights. Jackson's face seeped into my thoughts like a virus. I had no vaccine for him, but I wasn't going to let him destroy this moment.

"Trent..." I hesitated. What was I going to say?

"Ivy, I would like to apologize for earlier. Jackson and I... we don't really see eye to eye on things, especially for our kind and how we live," he said.

"He's always trying to control me," I confessed.

"Because you're not like any dhampir we've seen. You're incredible."

My heart swooned like a bird taking flight for the first time. "Really?"

Trent pushed all the food aside and scooted closer until he was right in front of me. His hands were placed on my cheeks so I could look directly at him.

"When I first saw you in the rec room, I knew you were special. I saw who you truly are. I want you," Trent declared.

Everything around us began to blur as my sights laser focused on his face. Trent's hazel eyes sparkled in the moonlight, eyeing me and then my lips. It was as if all the trouble he'd caused prior meant nothing. It became childish to even think to hold a grudge against him for wanting me to enjoy myself. Maybe he did see me for who I truly was, and Jackson was only holding me back so I wouldn't outshine the rest. My gut gave a little twig of some warning, but I ignored it. I wanted to trust Trent, and tonight proved I could. The only issue was, could I trust myself?

Trent leaned forward, stopping just before my lips. "I wanted to make up for the first time I kissed you. It wasn't proper." His breath tickled my face, making it a little harder to breathe.

"Show me."

And just like that, Trent closed the distance with his mouth planted gently on mine. It started out slow, teasing almost. He was gentle, which surprised me, and his hands never left my face. Our lips moved in perfect sync, soft and sweet. My hands ended up around his shoulders, pulling him in closer. It was delicate, as if he was being careful with me. I felt safe in this moment with him. His lip ring clinked against my teeth as he deepened the kiss, slipping his tongue through just enough to brush against mine. Everything became hot, and somehow, I ended up laying down on the blanket with him on top of me. Our bodies fused together from the heavy kissing, and I could feel something hard against my private area. Eventually, we needed to come up for air, so Trent pulled back slightly, our intake of breaths staggered.

"You taste good," he purred.

Goosebumps rose on both my arms, giving me away. Our foreheads pressed together, the tips of our noses touching. What just happened could only get better from here, and it made my heart do a few somersaults. Trent brushed my hair away from my face and stole one more kiss before getting off me. I sat up and smoothed out my outfit and sat back in a crossed-legged style. Trent grabbed my hand, and for the rest of the little dinner, we laughed and drank a whole bottle of wine, his eyes never leaving mine.

It wasn't until I got back inside, after kissing Trent one more time goodnight, that I noticed my door was slightly open. There, sitting on my bed with two pints of ice cream, was Gypsy, a look that could only mean she knew what I'd been doing displayed on her face.

"Hi," I breathed.

"Well, you look like you had a wild night," she said with a smirk.

I laughed a little too loud, making myself jump. I kicked off my shoes and joined Gypsy on the bed, snuggling under the covers.

"You have sex hair. Wait... did you have sex!" she exclaimed.

"Oh god, no!"

"Then why do you look like you went through a windstorm?"

"Trent and I... uh..." *What the fuck do I say?*

"NO FUCKING WAY!"

From there I went into a whole play by play of the night's events with Gypsy. Her expressions and gasps were priceless whenever I mentioned Trent and the kisses. There were moments she had to stop me and fan herself before I went on, and she would meow whenever I commented on Trent's eyes or touch.

"Wait!" Gypsy held up her hand, stopping me in my tracks.

"Yeah?"

"Jackson."

Even his name still gave me a feeling deep within. "What about him?"

"Do not play dumb with me."

I sighed. I really didn't want to go down this road with Gypsy. Jackson was my trainer, that was it. He was with Rebecca, and there was nothing I could do about it, no matter how badly, buried deep inside, my soul craved his touch, him and I were never going to be. "He's with Rebecca, that's it. Nothing to discuss."

She looked at me, pursing her lips. Gypsy then held up her hands for surrender, accepting my clipped response, and went back to asking details of the night with Trent. I exhaled internally with relief when I suddenly remembered I'd never opened the text from Jackson he'd sent earlier. *I'll look at it later,* I thought.

"Soon enough, you're going to do the nasty with Trent." Gypsy wiggled her eyebrows at me, making it pretty obvious she was talking about sex.

We laughed, and she handed me a pint of chocolate ice cream with a silver spoon and told me it was girls' night and she was sleeping over.

"Can we fit on this bed?" I questioned.

"We can't cuddle?" Her tone sounded like she was offended.

"We can, but I think one of us is going to fall off," I laughed.

"Good point. I'm going to request to get queen size beds for us."

About half a pint of ice cream later, Gypsy said it was time to discuss our basement escapade.

"An older gentleman was in this memory when I touched the mark. I was sitting on his lap, and I called him grandpa," I explained. My mind wandered back to that moment, back to his face.

"Woah, okay, so the mark is definitely a trigger for you," she said. Gypsy leaned forward, resting her chin on her hand, lost in thought.

"The mark was on his right forearm and I touched it. Gypsy, this mark is related to me somehow. It can't be a coincidence that it's appearing to me now."

"Do you know who the guy is?"

I reached for the lost vampire race book and turned to the page I'd left the red ribbon on. Kaspar Lane's photo stood out to me instantly, I pointed to his photograph, showing Gypsy. I watched her mouth the words to his name and eye the photo, scanning every square inch.

"Could this be your grandpa?" she whispered.

I shrugged. "I don't know. There are holes missing from my own life."

We sat in silence for a while, flipping through the book for any other leads that could potentially help us. Most pages left us at dead ends, never really explaining cause of death or who was the next of kin. It became pretty clear it was a family tree, an organized family tree. About midway through the book, we gave up and curled underneath the covers together, staring up at the ceiling.

"Ivy," she said.

"Yes?"

"Don't get mad...."

I propped myself up on my elbow, eager to hear what she had to say. Gypsy stared at the ceiling, avoiding my face.

"I know this won't change anything because now you and Trent are an item, but a little while ago, I overhead Jackson and Rebecca arguing outside his truck. They broke up."

I rolled back over to my side and shut my eyes. "Is that all?"

"Yes. Goodnight."

The bed shifted as Gypsy rolled over on her side.

Jackson was single. For a brief moment, I'd thought I was out of the clear with him. Free to roam as I pleased and had accepted our destiny. All I wanted was to get ahold of this dhampir life and get to know Trent better, but instead, life decided to throw me a curve ball to test my patience. Could that be what Jackson had texted me earlier? I highly doubted that but was still a bit curious to know. I snagged my phone from the bedside table and clicked on his text.

Jackson: Training is cancelled for tomorrow.

Good, now I can sleep, I thought. Not one mention of the breakup made it a little more bearable to face him tomorrow. I would be lying to myself if I claimed I didn't feel a little happy from the news, but would it change how he felt about me? I had just made out with Trent tonight, and even though he didn't claim me, I owed it to him to stay true to him only. Trent had seen my worth from the very beginning, Jackson saw me as a baby he was forced to babysit without pay. Here I thought I had everything figured out, and I might be back at square one. This would happen when I finally started to pursue someone else. I pulled the covers up higher to my chin and tried to let sleep take me away from this nightmare.

CHAPTER 20

Friday was my last shift before the weekend, and because it was Friday, at work, we ordered food for lunch and threw a little party whenever we completed a successful shipment and order. Patricia mentioned she would be gone all of next week, since she chose to take a trip to Canada with her husband to spend time with her relatives. I wished her safe travels and looked forward to hearing all about it when she returned.

Trent had been texting me nonstop during my shift, asking me how my day was going and when could we meet up again. We had a few different conversations, always leading back to flirting and teasing each other. The feelings he gave me distracted me, in a good way.

I said my goodbyes and wished everyone a fun weekend, waving obnoxiously through Elaine's office at Gypsy as she stuck her tongue out at me. She usually stayed until six, that gave me enough time to settle down before she hounded me on more questions about the texts with Trent.

As usual, I sent out a message to Jackson, letting him know I was ready to leave. His responses were usually quick, but ten minutes had passed, and I still hadn't heard from him. Deciding not to stand there by myself like an idiot, curiosity got the better of me, and I took a stroll through downtown. Since the formula had changed in the blood they gave me, I was able to withstand longer periods of time around humans before the hunger crept in. This gave me a chance to explore the town and not want to feed on every person who walked two feet from me. I took a walk down the same side of the street as the factory and began my exploration through town.

All the stores were lined up perfectly on either side of the road, and just a few feet in front of me was a cute little flower shop. Some flowers were secured in brown pots, others in elegant bouquets. Display upon display of flowers were showcased in front of the store, giving off smells like nothing I had experienced before. A guy was sniffing through a section of flowers, most likely trying to find the freshest set. There was a small grocery store placed neatly in between two three-story apartment buildings with people going in and out carrying brown paper bags. The closer I got to the center, the more congested it became with people. Couples holding hands, children screaming with laughter in a nearby park, and a group of teenage girls shopping together. It felt like a perfect scene out a movie, too good to be true. In complete awe with everything and wondering if I had participated in this sort of lifestyle before my transformation, I came across a pole with tons papers pinned to it. Colorful papers displayed yard sales, dance lessons at a nearby studio called Tiptoes, and a carnival was coming into town next week. I shifted through all the papers, reading the descriptions, when I froze at a familiar face on a plain white sheet.

My knees became weak and my breathing shallow, as I read the first line in bold letters:

Missing Person. Ivy Elizabeth Lane.

The photograph was me in a white blouse, smiling with rosy cheeks. My mouth became dry like a desert when I continued to read the next few lines.

Last seen October 15th, 2019 Auburn hair, green eyes. Height 5'5. Weight: 125. DOB: June 1st. 2000. If anyone has any information, please contact the number below.

My eyes traveled to the bottom of the paper and found it was torn at the end, only displaying two numbers.

Someone is looking for me, I thought. *Someone believes I'm still alive.*

I unpinned the paper and folded it until it could fit into my back pocket. Afraid to think there could be more, I continued down the road, searching each pole to see if another was pinned. So far, I just found the one on this side of the street and crossed safely over to check out the other poles. Still nothing, I came to a halt when I spotted Jackson a few hundred feet down on the opposite side of where I was. He was with a short man with a thick mustache, talking urgently. Both seemed to be engrossed in a deep conversation, always looking around, making sure nobody could hear. The mysterious, shorter man pulled out a brown envelope from inside his jacket and handed it to Jackson. He looked around before peeking inside, nodding at the man to confirm whatever was inside he had delivered as promised.

I took a couple steps back and broke out into a run back to the factory. I could not process what had just happened. My eyes were definitely playing tricks on me, and the flyer in my pocket burned as a reminder of what I had just witnessed. Catching my breath, I made it back just in time to make it look like I'd just stepped outside as Jackson pulled forward with his truck. Shaking the uneasy feeling in my bones, I hopped inside his truck and buckled myself in.

"How was work?" he asked, putting the truck in drive and speeding off down the road.

"The usual," I mumbled, afraid to give myself away with all the anxiety attacking me.

He nodded, staring straight ahead. "Sorry about cancelling last night, something came up. I thought maybe tonight we could begin the new workout routine. What do you say?"

"Sure thing, boss," I replied too quickly. I could feel him looking at me from the corner of my eye. *Shit, I blew my cover*, I thought. The paper, still burning in my pocket.

"Okay."

I let out a breath I was holding in and rested my head on the window, watching the trees blur from the truck's speed.

Parting ways with Jackson had become surprisingly easy when we exited his vehicle. I gave a quick see you later and dashed inside before he questioned me further. I ran up the stairs two at a time and entered my room safely without being stopped by anyone; a huge miracle if you asked me. I unfolded the paper from my pocket and placed it flat on my bed, then I grabbed the book where my supposed grandpa was documented next to it and opened to the page where his picture resided. The common thread to the both of us was now clear as day and it gave me chills just looking at it. Our last names were the exact same; spelling and all. *Lane*, I thought. So simple, yet I had no recollection of it. The photo they used gave me a weird feeling and did not showcase who I was today. Whoever my past self-had been, was no longer there. I'd grown into a completely different person, supernatural creature, to be exact. The girl in the photo staring back at me had promise and probably a bright future, the girl now, had holes and constant struggles. I envied my old self.

I went back and forth between my photo and my supposed grandfather and tried to pick out some similarities we could possibly have. The only thing I took real notice of was the shape of our eyes; big and full of life. I tucked the paper inside the page where Kaspar Lane had been placed and closed the book, slipping it right under my mattress for safe keeping.

Most of the details I desperately wanted to find were all on that one piece of paper. My height, weight, eye color, hair color, even my date of birth. I pushed the blanket aside on my bed and laid my head down on the pillow, swallowing as much of the information as I could. Nineteen years old, nineteen. That's how old I was. Then other thoughts came into play like, did I go to prom? Graduate high school? Get my license? Apply to college? College. Was I even in college? To be taken away and having barely lived started to piss me off. This all stemmed from the same burning question—why was I chosen? The biggest problem was Theodore and his shitty attendance. I had so many questions for him, and it seemed to be incredibly convenient he was out of town ninety-nine-point-nine percent of the time. Always on business trips, always having an excuse to not see or talk to me. He was the sole reason of who I was now, and he could not give a single fuck.

Tears rolled down my cheeks and hit the sheet on the mattress, creating a wet spot. My phone kept going off from texts, mostly like from Trent, but I ignored all of them. If he saw me like this, he might assume Jackson had something to do with me crying, and he would have gone looking for him; a disaster in the making.

A couple of hard knocks on my door and the sound of Trent's voice got me to wipe my tears and hide all traces of distress on my face quick enough when he began to call out to me.

"Ivy, I know you're in there," he said.

Giggling to myself, I spared Trent from his concerned hounding and opened the door to find him holding a bouquet of roses and a vial of blood. He smiled at me and held out the vial of blood first.

"Don't worry, I didn't tamper with this one," he reassured.

I snorted.

"Thank God." I took the vial and polished it off with one giant sip.

"Roses for my lady," Trent said. He took the vial from my hands and replaced it with the gorgeous bouquet. I leaned in to inhale the wonderful scent that radiated off the petals, completely blown away by his kind gesture.

"Thank you. They're lovely. Would you like to come in?" I moved aside to showcase my average room.

Trent bowed like a knight and took my hand, flipping it over to kiss my palm "Yes, I would love too." His sweet gesture left me breathless by the door.

"It's cute," he chuckled. I rolled my eyes and walked past him leaving the bouquet of flowers on my wooden dresser.

"I don't care for the extra stuff," I said.

Trent came over to me and wrapped his arms around my waist, kissing me lightly on the lips. "One of the many things I like about you."

"Woah, don't let me interrupt."

I tried to push out of Trent's arms, but he had me locked in place.

Rebecca leaned casually against the threshold of my bedroom, smiling at the sight of us. "Couldn't have Jackson, so you settled for Trent. How precious."

"Lost, Rebecca?" asked Trent.

"Nope. Never lost." She gave us one last look, turning on her heels and leaving my room.

I finally broke free from Trent's grasp and shut my bedroom door. "I can't stand her."

"Just ignore her. I do," he said.

If only it were that simple. "I try, believe me."

"Hey, are you doing anything tonight?"

"Training with Jackson."

"After that?"

"Uh... I don't know." I was caught off guard from his questions. *What was he planning?*

"I have a surprise. Just let me know if you're available later."

"Okay." Trent met me by the door and kissed me before leaving me as confused as ever.

Another thought hit me; Rebecca saw Trent and I in a romantic embrace. Rebecca and Jackson may be over, but who knows who she was going to tell. I was not ready to tell Jackson myself, and she could ruin everything. One thing is said and it all spreads like wildfire, and I was about to be swallowed whole. If only I'd gotten some type of warning when becoming a dhampir, I could've avoided all this crap.

CHAPTER 21

I threw on a fresh pair of workout clothes, tied my shoes up tight, and walked downstairs to the foyer to meet Jackson for our new workout. He had his arms crossed, eyeing me the whole way down each step. In a pair of gray sweats and white tee-shirt, he looked more like he was ready for bed then an actual workout.

"Ready," I announced when I reached the last step.

"Alright, follow me," he said.

Jackson led the way out the front door with me close on his heels.

Instead of turning the usual left to the field, Jackson turned right and saw the confused look on my face. "We built a fieldhouse months ago, it's this way."

This place was crawling with paths, and we stepped on another one, following it all the way down to a brick building. It was an underwhelming structure on the outside, simple exterior, a few planted bushes in the front. Jackson jogged up the front steps and unlocked the doors, holding it for me to walk through. He took the lead again and led me down a well-lit hallway, the smell of sweat and damp towels clung to the air. We reached the last door directly at the end, and he opened it up and had me step through first.

If I was being honest, I wasn't expecting it to be so spacious inside. A track circled the perimeter of the gym and in the dead center was a boxing ring. There were bleachers on either side, and toward the back wall stood some machinery, my guess workout equipment, all in a row.

"We're going to box today," he announced.

I gulped. "Are you sure?"

Jackson could sense my uneasiness and laughed. "Yes, you'll be fine. We'll start out slow."

He walked over to a long table set up just outside the ring. It held two sets of gloves and mouthguards. Jackson handed me the mouthguard and then the gloves, helping me put them on one at a time. They felt tight with my hands inside, and I was afraid my hands were going to be permanently stuck. Jackson grabbed his pair and headed over to the ring, forgetting his mouthguard, and lifted the rope to make a space wide enough for me to go through. Once I stepped into the ring, anxiety kicked in a little. Jackson put on his gloves but disregarded his mouthpiece.

"Okay, let's begin," he said.

I stood there in an awkward stance not knowing what to do. "Uh, yeah about that."

"Relax, I'm going to show you the proper technique."

"Fantastic," I groaned.

He ignored me and continued with his lesson. "To start, we will begin with your stance. It's easy." Jackson stood next to me on my left, feet spread apart, "your left foot should be forward. Next, make sure your right foot is in a ninety-degree angle. Imagine a line in between your legs. Front toe, back heel on the imaginary line." Jackson changed his footing to exactly what he described. I mimicked to the best of my ability, "excellent, now, the key to good foot placement, is to always have your right foot partially lifted off the ground. It keeps the weight toward the front and a better swing in the end," Jackson lifted his right foot just enough to hover off the ground and swung with his right arm to show the precision of his proper stance, "always keep your weight toward the front. Once you have that down, make sure your knees are bent, this is when power and balance come into play," He bent his knees, which gave himself a little bounce. I copied him, more confident than when I first started. "Your shoulders and arms should be relaxed. Eventually, with practice, you will become accustomed to your own stance, and it will flow more naturally."

Jackson went back over to his side and got into his own stance. "Put your mouthpiece in," he ordered.

I did as he said and stuck the rubber mouthguard in my mouth. Jackson smiled, and that's when I realized he lacked his own mouthguard. Cocky as he was, I'd never seen him so relaxed and confident. Making sure my stance lined up with his, I relaxed my shoulders and arms, and I was ready to begin.

"Okay. I want you to take the first hit at me," instructed Jackson.

In one swift motion, I swung my right arm at his jaw. He dodged effortlessly, making me stagger back out of place.

"Don't let my dodges deter you from your confidence. Get back in formation, bend your knees, and do it again."

I repeated the same swing with my right arm, only when Jackson dodged, I swung my left up without warning and collided with his cheek. He didn't budge an inch from his spot, but he had a surprised look on his face from my combo.

"That was good. Let's go again."

For the next thirty minutes, Jackson would let me swing in different sets of combos, and at least five out of the ten I tried, hit him in the face. By the end of the match, our bodies were soaked with sweat. Jackson and I cleaned up our mess and made plans to do this again for our next workout. He praised me on how quickly I learned, and that he'd never met anyone who could remember their own combos that easily. I could smell the rain before I reached the door, the sound penetrated from the roof. Thunder rolled in with each flash of lighting that struck whatever nearby area, causing lights to flicker in the fieldhouse.

"On the count of three we run. One... two... three," Jackson yelled.

We both booked it out the door, the rain soaking us within minutes.

I screamed with excitement, and Jackson laughed hysterically until we got into the main foyer. We were completely drenched, dripping on the hardwood floors.

"I need to get out of these clothes," I commented.

He laughed as I made my way up to my bedroom.

Our shoes squeaked like ducks with each step we took and had us laughing whenever one of us did it the loudest. My bedroom was warm, and I couldn't wait to get out of the wet clothes. I pulled open my drawers and rummaged through its contents, trying to find something warm to wear. Jackson leaned against the threshold, arms crossed, his blond hair dripped from his scalp to the floor. His soaked, white tee clung to his body, outlining his muscles and v-line. I found a regular black t-shirt and gray sweats, about to throw them on, when I realized Jackson was still watching me.

"Do you mind?" I asked.

"It's nothing I haven't seen before. Don't flatter yourself baby dhamp," he said matter-of-factly.

I rolled my eyes. "Just because you're single, doesn't mean you get a free show."

"Who told you I was single?"

I stiffened. I forgot Gypsy gave me all the good gossip, and I wasn't supposed to know any of those personal details. I turned around and avoided his intense stare, waiting for him to go away. My bedroom door clicked shut as Jackson's footsteps creaked behind me on the floor. *Shit.* Somehow, the air changed around us. My pulse quickened with each step he took forward until I could feel his breath on the back of my neck. My skin ignited when his fingertips lightly caressed my arm. The clothes I had in my hand fell to the floor, I was paralyzed by him. Any thought of Trent was evaporated as soon Jackson touched me. I know I should tell him about kissing Trent, but my mouth was dry, and I couldn't form the words. I was completely under Jackson's spell.

"Interesting... how your skin reacts to me," Jackson murmured.

I gulped. "You don't feel the same." It wasn't a question. I knew he didn't feel the same, even with Rebecca out of the picture.

His other hand gripped my waist, his fingers imprinted into my skin through my soaked shirt. His mouth brushed lightly against my neck. "Why do you assume that?"

"Because, it's how you act," I stated, losing my strength to concentrate.

"Mmmm,"

His soft lips grazed my neck down to my collarbone. My breath hitched in the back of my throat when he whipped me around to face him. Jackson's eyes smoldered under the lights as he tucked a piece of my hair behind my ear. Jackson leaned in, waiting for me to follow suit. It was then my mouth decided to be honest and tell him the truth.

"I kissed Trent," I confessed.

Jackson froze, his eyes burning with anger. "When?"

"The other day."

"Why?"

"Why? Because...I don't know. I kind of like him."

He stepped back from me, a look of disgust on his face. "He's a piece of shit, Ivy. You can't trust him."

"Oh, but I can trust you?"

"Yeah, you can!"

I leaned over and began to laugh, "That's rich. You don't realize how you treat me."

A look of disbelief plastered his face. "Treat you? Ivy, you don't understand."

"Oh, I understand."

Jackson ran his hands through his hair in a frustrated manner. "Ivy, listen to yourself! Trent has secrets..."

"Jackson, do you *hear* yourself?! You're just as guilty with secrets!"

He sat down on my bed and covered his face with his hands, sighing deeply. I crossed my arms and watched his shoulders slouch in defeat. There was no way in hell I was going to let him be right. Still drenched from the rain, I picked up my clothes and headed towards the door.

"Ivy," he said.

My hand, inches from the doorknob, dropped when he said my name. "Jackson."

His smooth hands touched my arms, turning me around to face him. "There's so much I want to tell you, believe me, but I'm tightly bound."

"Well, let's start to unwind that. I need the truth, Jackson. I'm tired of being in the dark."

Jackson reached forward to cup my cheek, caressing my flushed skin with his thumb. I leaned in, suddenly overwhelmed by everything happening around me. "Please," I whispered.

"Ivy..."

"Ivy! Girl, open up we gotta talk!" Gypsy shouted.

Jackson froze, our eyes locked. *This could not be happening*, I thought.

A wave of sadness came over me when Jackson dropped his hand and stepped back. Just when I thought we were going to make progress with being truthful, an interruption happens. My heart was still beating hard against my ribcage, the sound pulsating to my eardrums.

Jackson surprised me by placing a finger to his lips to let me know I needed to be quiet and leaned in for a kiss on my forehead. He broke it off too soon and opened my door to see Gypsy standing there with both hands on her hips. He walked by her as if she didn't exist. Gypsy turned to me, her mouth wide open in shock. I shoved her inside before she opened her mouth and started asking questions.

"Ivy..." she paused, her mouth still agape.

"Gypsy, if we could just refrain right now, that would be grand," I breathed, my mind completely clouded with thoughts of Jackson.

"Fine, but you owe me later," whined Gypsy. She jumped and landed her butt on the end of my bed, pouting like a five-year-old.

"You said you wanted to talk?" I reminded her.

She cocked her head to the side as if to recall something far away she couldn't reach. "I forgot."

A heavy sigh escaped my lips and I decided to join her on my bed. "Perfect."

"Anything new?"

Tapping my chin, I tried to summon anything new I needed to show her in my ever-confused head, then I remembered about the flyer with my face on it.

"Yeah, I do," I finally said.

Grabbing the book underneath the mattress, I pulled out the flyer from one of the pages I had tucked it in and handed it to Gypsy. She unfolded the paper and I watched her expression change from muddled to what the fuck.

CHAPTER 22

"Is this real?" she questioned. Gypsy kept flipping the piece of paper over, double checking to see if what she saw was true.

"I found that not too far from the factory. Whoever is looking for me, believes I'm still alive," I added.

"It also means, they're not too far from you either."

Suddenly, all the pieces began to fuse together. "I don't think I ever truly left."

I had a plan formulating in my head when Gypsy read my description, "It's October 29th today and this says you've been missing since October 15th."

"Yes, I suppose that is the date I went missing," I mumbled.

"It's a big clue! So what are we going to do?"

When I began to establish a plan, Gypsy was not in the equation. This was the part I was dreading the most. "Gypsy...."

"Aww why can't I come!"

"I don't want you in trouble with the council." I patted her shoulder as her big eyes gave me her ultimate puppy-dog stare.

"I need your help here. This has to be a solo mission," I explained. Silently praying she understood, I watched as her expression changed from sad to understanding.

"Alright. What is it you need me to do?"

The plan was simple. Gypsy already had the address in hand, and I would uber there under Gypsy's account so nothing would trace back to me. She was also going to cover my absence—I was more afraid of how Trent was going to react. Shit, Trent. I couldn't think about that now. Especially since I was supposed to text him later. Shit, again.

I would then investigate the area and scope out if anyone was posting new flyers. If I couldn't find anyone doing that, then I was going to confront the man Jackson had been conversing with and demand to know what was going on. I highly doubted the man had any connection to me, but it wouldn't hurt to try and fish for more information. We said our goodbyes and agreed to meet up around eight pm in the foyer.

Jeans, a sweatshirt, and a baseball cap was the outfit of choice to investigate. I had to hide myself somehow while hunting for clues in a town I barely knew. I took a couple deep breaths, preparing myself for the worst, but hoping for the best. Gypsy was right where she said she would be at 8 pm, hanging out downstairs. She saw me come down the stairs and met me on the last step, grabbing ahold of my arm.

"The Uber is here, and it'll take you to the factory. Call me if anything happens. I have my car ready to go in case you need me," she said. Gypsy gave me a tight hug, almost knocking the wind out of me.

"I'll be fine. Just make sure Jackson and Trent can't find me," I reminded her.

She nodded and walked me to the front door and watched me get into a black, sleek Honda. I waved goodbye from the window and leaned my head back against the seat, trying to control the anxiety creeping in.

The trees blurred with each passing moment we got further away from the mansion, my hands became clammy, and I had to wipe them on my jeans to dry them up. Deep down inside, I wasn't ready to find out the truth, but I knew in my gut I had to know. The what ifs replayed like a terrible sitcom intro song, and I reminded myself that no matter what happened, this could be worse. The guy who drove the black Honda played soft classical music, and it smelt like sweet mint and stale tobacco on the seats. He would look at me through his mirror and smile awkwardly with his missing teeth. Getting antsy by each passing minute, the trees finally diminished, and the town lines came into my view. Halloween was approaching, so all the stores were decorated with pumpkins, ghosts, and witches. It was the beginning of the weekend, but because it was so late, all shops were closed up for the night. It was a good sign—I could focus more and not be so distracted and tempted by walking blood bags.

The Uber driver pulled up to the front of the factory and wished me a good day as I got out and took a deep breath. From what I remembered, I went back toward the center of town and passed by the grocery store and flower shop. Following the same path as before, I casually strolled down the street and took my time at each pole with pinned flyers on it, double checking to see if any new flyers of myself were added to the group. So far, the poles were bare of my face, and I passed by the pole where I found the one I'd taken yesterday.

The closer I got to where I'd seen Jackson with the man, the more disappointed I became with zero new information I could bring back. Feeling discouraged, I found a bench near a small park off to the right and sat myself down, taking a mini break to recollect my thoughts and plans. Chills ran down my spine as the wind picked up, and a small pile of leaves near a drainage swirled up in the air. I observed the vacant town, surprised by how quiet everything seemed. An empty playground was behind me. The moon lit up parts of the slides and swings, and I could picture kids from earlier in the day running around.

Debating on whether to give up and go looking for the mystery man, I scanned my surroundings from the bench one last time, getting a good look around me. Just then, not too far from where I sat, on the opposite side of the road, I spotted Jackson walking to each pole, ripping a specific piece of paper off and crumpling it up. He did this to each pole—stopped, looked over his shoulder, checking around him, and then trashed it. He walked further down the street, and I made a split-second decision to run over and see what he'd tossed out. I dug deep in the trash, finding that one piece of paper he had rolled up into a ball. I reached for it and tried to smooth out the mess. My face smiled back at me just as it had the day before, haunting me. All this time, even now, everything seemed to make sense for the first time since I woke up. Anger boiled beneath the surface, and no matter how many times I tried to tell myself to calm down, I remembered everything that led up to this point.

Of course, if I was smart, I would've ran back to the factory, called the Uber, and gotten the hell out of there, but that wasn't the case anymore. Jackson needed to be confronted, and answers had to be met before I did anything rash. I stood there, watching him finish disposing of the last of the evidence, when he turned around and we locked eyes. The world around me spun faster than any carnival ride could ever achieve. Pain and betrayal were two common emotions that engulfed my heart, making my chest ache. Jackson stepped forward as I stepped back, now afraid to even look at him. He noticed my action and sprinted forward, trying to reach me. I dashed back across the street to a now empty park and ran over to the swing set, leaning against the metal structure. Not a few seconds later, Jackson's heavy footsteps made his presence known, and I just couldn't take it anymore.

It was suddenly very clear to me that Jackson had known who I was the whole time. My slow heart felt heavy, almost to the point where it could drop into my stomach at any moment. Jackson's soft gray eyes grew wide with concern as I continued to stay silent to control my emotions. He stepped toward me, and I mirrored a step back. He ran his soft, big hand through his untucked blond hair, biting his lower lip.

I swallowed a hard lump in my throat before I spoke. "You knew."

"Ivy... I," he whispered.

"You knew who I was the whole goddamn time, and you didn't tell me?" I snapped. My blood began to boil over its limit.

"Ivy! It was not that simple!" he fired back.

Everything around me seemed to be closing in, invisible walls started to push forward on me, making it harder to breathe. "I don't believe you."

Jackson's eyes became wild with despair as he stepped forward and grabbed my hand. "I never wanted to hurt you."

"Well you did one fucking outstanding job."

"I had a code to follow! You think I wanted this? Any of it!" he shouted.

I ripped my hand from his, "You're a lying sack of shit, Jackson!"

"Am I? Ivy! Is that all you got to fucking say? I have done nothing but help you through all of this, and then you go ahead and call me a liar?"

"I didn't ask for this! I didn't want to be this... this... monster!"

"You're more than that, Ivy," mumbled Jackson.

"You're right. I am more than that. I'm better. I deserve better. I deserve the fucking truth, and if I can't get it here, I'm going to find it somewhere else," I ran down the street, away from Jackson and his lies.

My anger was at an all-time high, and my hunger was escalated even more. I ran until the road widened and revealed a few businesses on either side. The sky boasted bright stars, and bats flapped aggressively overhead. I scanned the sidewalk and street, trying to find a different path to take and hopefully someone to drain. The thought made my mouth watered to the point of drool escaping at the corners of my lips. I needed to drink. No. I *wanted* to drink. I was angry and heated from all the truth coming undone before me, I wanted to feed until the pain in my chest and soreness in my throat were soothed by the thick, beautiful crimson blood touching my tongue. The farther I got into town, the harder it was to find anyone around. I kept scanning the streets and sniffed the air in between stops, trying to catch a whiff of anything related to blood. I never ate an animal before, the thought wasn't completely appeasing, but it would do if that was all I could find.

Eventually, I ended up near an abandon house with bordered up windows and a foreclosed sign on the front lawn. I stopped and sat down on the grass and tried to calm myself down. It was then I saw a young girl leave a small little brick house with a stack of papers in her hands from across the way. I watched her pin a piece of paper from the stack onto a light post, surprised she hadn't noticed me staring at her. I spoke to soon. The wind picked up, filling my lungs with a delicious smell, a smell so potent my mouth was watering. Our eyes locked, and instantly and I got a sudden wave of familiarity in my chest. Her face changed to utter shock and started to run toward me, dropping the stack of papers to the ground.

"IVY! IT'S ME! HAZEL! OH MY GOD, I CAN'T BELIEVE I FOUND YOU!" she shouted with excitement. As she approached me, tears stained her rosy cheeks. Her pulse penetrated through her soft, ivory skin, exposing a beautiful thick vein. My mouth began to water.

"Ivy, where have you been?" she questioned.

I finally made contact with her soft hazel eyes and felt another wave of familiarity. *Why is she so familiar?* I thought. She leaned forward and gave me a big bear hug. Her scent was of floral and sweat, but her blood was just underneath a few layers of skin, calling to me.

"My god, girl. You've been gone for over two weeks! Griffin and I have been looking everywhere for you! Your parents are going to be so happy. They all thought you were dead, but I didn't believe it. They had a funeral and everything. What the hell happened to you? And why are you so quiet?" asked Hazel.

"IVY!" shouted Jackson from down the street.

Hazel peeked over my shoulder to track down the voice that was screaming my name. "Who is that?"

This girl Hazel wasn't making any sense to me with all these questions. Apparently, I had parents, and she knew them. And who the hell was Griffin? The sense of knowing her was there, but it didn't feel right; not anymore. My hunger bubbled up in my throat, causing an ache that needed to be soothed. I tried to push the thoughts out, but it got worse whenever she moved.

I could hear Jackson's footsteps getting closer, afraid I wouldn't have enough time to feed.

"You okay? Ivy, my god, can you answer me or something!" she demanded.

"What were you doing over there?" I pointed to the scattered papers on the ground.

"Oh, I was adding your flyers back on the light posts. Some ass was taking them down," she answered. *Jackson*, I thought.

"Who's Griffin?"

"What? Ivy, that's my bro..."

Jackson came to a halt in front of Hazel, her attention averted to him, her eyes wild with confusion.

"Who the heck are you?" demanded Hazel, putting her hands on her hips.

"Does it matter who I am? Ivy let's go, now," he ordered.

Hazel took a step forward to block Jackson's path, "Get lost!"

"Ivy," he warned

"No." I finally said. Both Hazel and Jackson turned to look at me, surprised by my harsh no. I couldn't take it anymore, the hunger was overtaking my senses, and whoever I was to Hazel, had been destroyed.

Hazel turned back to Jackson with a smirk on her face. "See, she doesn't want to go either, now move it along, pretty boy."

221

I snaked my arms around Hazel in a tight grip, keeping her locked in place. She jumped in surprised, struggling against my hold. "Ivy...what are you doing?"

"Don't do this," he begged. Jackson took a step forward as I pushed Hazel's head to the side to expose her neck. How fitting that she wore an off the shoulder tee-shirt to expose her pretty, soft skin.

"You wanted a monster. So, here I am. I never wanted this life and now I'm taking charge like I should have done from the very beginning," I snapped. I took my pointer finger and slashed a thick laceration down Hazel's neck. She yelped in pain, still trying to break free.

"What the fuck is wrong with you?" she shouted.

"Ivy, stop!" croaked Jackson taking half a step toward us.

The blood from her open wound pooled out down the front of her shirt. The crimson red river painted her skin, and my mouth was drooling with anticipation. Jackson's eyes were filled with fear, but that didn't stop what I was about to do.

"If you do this... you can't go back," he said.

"Don't care." I gripped the other side of Hazels neck and brought my mouth to the wound I'd made. She tasted like sweet candy, but better. It filled my body; it gave me strength and pleasure all in one. My adrenaline became heightened with each sip I took from her. I could feel her squirm under my touch, fighting to break free. I gripped harder, digging my nails in her skin, exposing more blood. I drank and drank until my body felt on fire, blazing from my toes to the top of my head. I could feel myself growing stronger, my body reacting to her blood in a positive way. My muscles felt stronger, my mind was clearer. I could hear better and smell better too. I drained and drained until her body became limp in my arms. I collapsed on the sidewalk with her until I finished. My whole body was on fire with new senses and strength. I let go and placed her head gently on the ground. Jackson kneeled down in front of us, placing two fingers by her neck to check her pulse.

"She's gone," he announced, not sounding shocked at all.

I stared at her soft face, she looked almost peaceful.

"We have to remove the body and then get out of here before someone sees us," said Jackson. He began to lift Hazel's lifeless body as I licked my fingers clean.

"Hazel! Where are you?" shouted a male voice.

Jackson froze just as I did. I closed my eyes and tried to concentrate on the male that was near us. Suddenly, my body became weak and my head was clouded. I felt an overwhelming sensation to fall asleep.

"Jackson," I groaned. I tried to get myself to my feet, but my body was far too weak to hold itself up.

"Shit," Jackson whispered.

Jackson dropped Hazel back down on the ground and came over to me, lifting my face to meet his attention.

"You're changing. I need to get you out of here," said Jackson.

"Now?" I cried.

Jackson lifted me in his arms and ran me over to his truck that was parked next to an ice cream shop. He placed me gently on the passenger seat, making sure my head didn't hit the roof of the truck. My body sizzled all over like tiny little flames were lit on every surface of my skin. Sweat poured profusely down my face as I tried desperately to keep myself from going under. Just as Jackson buckled me in and shut the door, I could hear faintly that same male voice screaming for the woman named Hazel. Jackson got in and shifted gears to put the truck in reverse, trying to get us out of there as quickly as he could. My sweaty forehead was plastered to the window and my breathing came in shallow breaths, trying to hold on. There, near the foreclosed house where we left the poor lifeless girl, was a boy with beautiful curly hair bending over her body. In a split second, he looked up directly in my direction, our eyes locking. In the haze of my transformation, a look of recognition appeared on his face. But I did not recognize the boy, and as we drove off, I wondered if I would ever see him again.

ACKNOWLEDGEMENTS

To Hayley: without your constant support and guidance and faith in me, I would have never believed this could be possible, including everyone in the Notebook family.

To my parents: for your constant love and support since my birth. Mom, thank you for being you and teaching me how to be kind to others. Also, for giving the best hugs. Dad, my twin, thank you for showing me hard work does pay off and to never take anyone's crap. I love you both.

My siblings: Steven, Greg, Alysa, and Angela. For all the laughs, stupid sibling fights, and hugs. Each one of you hold a place in my heart, and I'm forever grateful to have you all by my side.

My nephew, Jon: I love you, nug. Although you won't know now, but when you read this someday, just know, having you as my godson was the best gift I received this year.

My Memere: my beautiful grandmother. Whose French accent never faltered over the years and who is a wonderful example of never giving up and just loving life. I love you always.

My godparents. Vaughn and Sandra: for showing me guidance and being selfless. The two strongest people I know and look up to. I love you.

My best friends. Brianna, Emily, Alyson, Chris, Zach, Gill, Brent, Pat, Tami, Katy, Teresa, Justin, Tyler, Vanessa, Ally, Alexis, Morgan, and Meghan: without you guys, and how amazing each of you are, the book might not have come to life.

To Justin M.: to the best guy friend out there who never stopped listening to me whine and complain about how awful I thought my work was. Thank you for being my anchor when it came to coming back to the writing world. Thank you, thank you, thank you.

And Jeff.